Love At First Flight

By Linda Shenton Matchett

Love at First Flight
By Linda Shenton Matchett

Cover Design and author photo by: Wes Matchett

PHOTO CREDITS: iStock/Tom Kelley Archive

ISBN-13: 978-1-7347085-6-1

Published by Shortwave Press

This is a work of fiction. Names, characters, places, and incidents either are the products of the author's imagination or are used fictitiously. Any resemblance to actual events or persons, living or dead, is entirely coincidental.

Praise for *Love at First Flight*

"Another excellent WWII novel where Shenton Matchett's expertise shines. Past heartache won't keep Evelyn Reid from becoming a top notch pilot, but when flight instructor Jasper MacPherson is reassigned to her post, Evelyn must decide if a second chance at love is worth altering her flight path." Barbara Britton, best-selling author, *Until June*

"*Love at First* Flight is a sweet second-chance Christian romance with a pinch of intrigue set against the backdrop of WWII WASP training missions. Good depiction of pilots, airplanes, and life on the air base. With characters you can root for, it's an enjoyable read." Award-winning author Jeanne M. Dixon, RITA award finalist *Grounded Hearts*

"Putting down this story is difficult, I can testify. While learning a great deal about the contribution of women pilots to the WWII cause, I spent a delightful few hours cheering on one of them. The obvious historical research and ongoing, realistic tension between the heroine and hero kept me totally involved." Gail Kittleson, Author, Women of the Heartland series

Dedicated to the thirty-eight WASP who lost their lives in the line of duty:

Champlin, Jane

Clarke, Susan P.

Davis, Margie L.

Dussaq, Katherine

Edwards, Marjorie D.

Erickson, Elizabeth

Fort, Cornelia

Grimes, Frances

Hartson, Mary

Howson, Mary H.

Keene, Edith

Lawrence, Kathryn B.

Lee, Hazel Ah Ying

Loop, Paula

Lovejoy, Alice

McDonald, Lea Ola

Martin, Peggy

Moffatt, Virginia

Moses, Beverly

Nichols, Dorothy

Norbeck, Jeanne L.

Oldenburg, Margaret

Rawlinson, Mabel

Roberts, Gleanna

Robinson, Marie N. (Mitchell)

Scott, Betty

Scott, Dorothy

Seip, Margaret J.

Severson, Helen Jo

Sharon, Ethel Marie

Sharp, Evelyn

Silver, Gertrude (Tompkins)

Stine, Betty P.

Toevs, Marion

Trebing, Mary E.

Webster, Mary L.

Weiz, Bonnie Jean

Wood, Betty L. (Taylor)

Chapter One

Evelyn Reid tightened her grip on the yoke of the BT-13 as the plane shimmied and roared. The aircraft wasn't called the Vultee Vibrator for nothing. She'd been in the air for about fifteen minutes in a practice run to build up hours toward receiving her qualification for the plane, and its rocking continued to increase.

Alone, she reveled in the majestic view high above the arid Texas landscape, so different from her native Wisconsin. Brown rather than green. Scrub trees rather than majestic quaking aspen or white cedar. No chance of seeing any sugar maples transform from Kelly green to flaming orange or red. The horizon stretched in front of her, the robin's-egg blue of the heavens dotted with puffy, marshmallow-like clouds. She smiled and relaxed against the seat. Oh, how she loved to fly.

Not all kids knew what they wanted to be when they grew up, but she'd never had any doubt. As a child, she'd watched the eagles and hawks soar overhead, dreaming of joining them in the sky. Then her parents took her to a barnstorming event, and she'd ridden in a rickety biplane. The experience confirmed her desire to be a pilot, and from that day forward she began to save every penny she earned for the day she'd be old enough to take lessons.

The Vultee's engine sputtered, and Evelyn's gaze shot to the instrument panel, studying each gauge for an indication of trouble. Nothing. The controls all registered normal. The ragged sputtering smoothed out…well, as smooth as the Vibrator ever got, and she blew out a deep breath.

A quick glance at her watch. Still twenty minutes remained of her flight. Just enough time to return to the base. With proficient motions, she turned the aircraft until the compass read northeast. Whistling Tommy Dorsey's latest number, she tapped her fingers on the control wheel in rhythm to the peppy song. She had the best job in the world. No doubt about it.

Her crop dusting business had been fun, guiding her yellow Piper Cub back and forth across the wide fields, but ferrying military aircraft gave her a thrill like nothing she'd ever experienced. The impressive size of the planes coupled with their enormous power sent excitement through her veins every time she boarded. She hadn't thought twice after receiving the telegram from Nancy Harkness Love two years ago inviting her to apply to her Women's Auxiliary Ferrying Squadron. Not long afterward, the WAFS had combined with Jackie Cochran's group to form the Women Air Service Pilots.

Evelyn didn't care what her unit was called as long as she was allowed to fly. Three weeks ago, she'd been selected for training in pursuit planes. Small, light, and fast, these aircraft acted as escort fighter planes for the bigger, cumbersome bombers. She'd already qualified in the P-39. Only a couple more runs in the Vultee, and she'd be ready for her check flight on the aircraft. Yep, she definitely had the best job in the world.

Coughing, the engine spewed black exhaust. The propeller faltered then continued to spin. Her breath hitched, and she pressed her lips together. Bucking and swaying, the aircraft pitched forward. She pulled up on the yoke and straightened her trajectory. In front of her the airport beckoned. Could she make it to the runway, or should she jump and ditch the plane? With a price tag of over twenty-three thousand dollars, the plane would be an expensive pile of rubbish if she let it crash.

She stiffened her spine and picked up the radio. "This is aircraft four-four-three-one-five-one-one, calling control tower. Please come in. Over."

"This is control tower. We see you, aircraft four-four-three-one-five-one-one. Are you in trouble? Over."

"Yes. Engine failing. I'm going to try to land her, so have the fire trucks ready. Over."

"Negative. Abandon the plane immediately. Over."

"I'm too low to eject, control tower. I'm going to bring her in. Just send the trucks. I'm heading for runway two. Over and out."

With a final gasp then a bang, the engine stalled, and the propeller froze, blades at the ten o'clock and two o'clock positions. *Thank You, God, for giving me visibility.* Evelyn narrowed her eyes and focused on the black strip of macadam that was her destination. Heavy in her hands, the plane continued to lose altitude as she struggled to keep it airborne until she reached the runway. Sweat formed at her hairline and slicked the skin beneath her goggles. Her blouse clung to her back under her jacket. Fingers cold and stiff, she fought with the aircraft. "Come on, don't fail me now. We can do this."

Please, God, I don't want to die.

Tiny specks grew larger then became buildings and vehicles. From her right, emergency trucks sped toward the end of the runway.

Three hundred feet.

Two hundred feet.

One hundred feet.

Fifty feet.

Bang!

The plane slammed into the ground then screeched and wailed as it hurtled forward. Belted into place, Evelyn's body pressed against the seat, her neck jerking with every movement of the aircraft. She mashed on the brakes, but the aircraft didn't slow. The landing gear was probably damaged or gone. The nose tipped forward and scraped the macadam. She released the wheel and threw her hands in front of her face. Glass shattered and spewed into the cockpit as the metal frame crumpled. There was nothing more she could do to control the plane. Heart hammering, she closed her eyes waiting for the end. Waiting for her life to be snuffed out in an instant.

Then the great beast decelerated until grinding to a halt inches before the end of the blacktop. Fingers trembling, she opened the seat belt then fumbled with the canopy's latch. She needed to get out. The crash might have torn the fuel lines. The aircraft could blow up at any time. She scraped her hands against the jagged glass and gasped. Blood coursed down her hands as she fought with the lock.

One final shove, and the bolt broke free. Yes! She thrust open the enclosure. A pair of strong arms reached in and hauled her up and over the edge of the cockpit. Her legs gave way, and she sagged against the firm body of her rescuer. He wrapped his arm around her waist and dragged her from smoking wreckage. The acrid smell of petroleum clung to the air.

She stumbled and fell to her knees, her hands scraping the rough ground. Breath heaving, she collapsed, face lying in the dirt. She was alive. Rolling over, her muscles protested every motion. She attempted to sit up, and a sharp pain knifed her side. Had she broken a rib?

The arms still supported her, and she scraped her hair away from her face to catch a glimpse of her guardian angel. Her jaw dropped. What was he doing here?

Jasper MacPherson knew the moment Evelyn recognized him. And she was obviously not happy that the past had shown up in the form of her ex-boyfriend. She pulled back and struggled to her feet.

He frowned. "You should remain seated until the medics have a chance to examine you."

"You're a doctor, now?" Venom coated her words. "I'm fine."

"No, you're not." He yanked a handkerchief from his pocket and tried to press it against the laceration on her forehead, but she turned her head, avoiding his ministrations. Fortunately, the wound didn't look deep, but she might have a concussion. "Don't be belligerent, Evelyn. There are protocols for a crash."

"I'll go to the infirmary. I don't need your help." She swayed, but maintained her balance.

He pressed the cloth into her fingers then shoved his hands into his pockets. Still the same stubborn girl he knew in college. Some things never change. "Why didn't you bail out? You could have been killed."

"There wasn't enough time. And at the price of these babies, I was hoping to salvage at least some of the parts." She tossed a glance at the burning aircraft and winced. "Apparently, I was unsuccessful."

"You always did think you were invincible, but one of these days you're going to be wrong."

"And you hope to be there, I assume. To grind my nose in my failure. Does that make you feel important, Jasper? Is it necessary to be right all the time and never make a mistake? Must be difficult to be perfect."

"I'm not—"

"Spare me your explanations, Jasper." Her gaze swept up and down his coverall-clad figure. "And your excuses as to why you and your mechanics can't manage to keep an aircraft in working order. This crash has nothing to do with pilot error and everything to do with a faulty plane."

A chill slithered up his spine. "What do you mean?"

"Just what I said. The engine ran rough then quit after belching black smoke. No amount of work on my part could bring the motor back to life. So I weighed my options and decided to bring her in." She poked his chest with her index finger. "This sort of thing wouldn't have happened if you boys knew what you were doing. Don't you read the manuals? Or do we have another problem? This isn't the first time me or the girls have had to deal with a defective aircraft, and I don't think the problem originates at the factory."

"You think there's sabotage involved?" His eyes widened. "Surely, not."

Her lips thinned. "Protecting your boys, are you? Think us girls don't know our stuff? When one of us gets killed because something is wrong with the plane, perhaps you'll take me seriously." She pivoted on her heels and rushed toward the hangar, her gait uneven.

Jasper turned and studied the crash site. The emergency crew had doused the ruins with the sodium bicarbonate-chemical mixture, and the smoke was beginning to dissipate. He shuddered at the jumbled mass of glass and metal then ran his hand across his crew cut. *Thank You, God, for keeping Evelyn safe during the crash.*

With his attire, she'd thought he was one of the mechanics. What would she say when she discovered he was one of her instructors? Probably quite a bit. She was never one at a loss for words. Perhaps he should put in for a transfer.

He huffed a sigh. The commanding officer would never go for it. He'd tell them to work out their personal differences and keep their eyes on the goals: to train pilots and ferry the planes. Tough to give a wide berth to a person when she was assigned to his class. Exhilaration and dread had warred for supremacy last night when he'd reviewed the rosters and spied her name on one of the lists. Now that they'd had their first interaction, he should have known dread was the appropriate response.

She looked good. Very good.

Even in a bedraggled uniform with her ebony hair a tangled mass and her porcelain skin scraped and bruised, Evelyn was a gorgeous woman. Intelligence crackled from her ice-blue eyes that changed colors depending on her mood. At five foot three, she barely qualified for the WASP height requirement, and she'd probably stuffed herself with bananas to meet the weight specification.

Scrubbing at his face with cold fingers, he straightened his spine. An army air force officer, he could keep his emotions under control, train her, and get her out of here. Hopefully, his heart wouldn't be too bruised by the end of her stay.

The idea of that transfer sounded better by the minute.

Chapter Two

Conversation ebbed and flowed in the mess hall as Evelyn eased herself into a vacant chair across the table from two WASP who'd arrived yesterday for training. Cleared by the medical officer, she regretted her decision to attend calisthenics this morning. Intent on proving to herself and everyone else she was fit for duty, she'd tried to outperform the instructor. Bad idea.

Her muscles protested with her every move, but she schooled her features not to wince. She put down her tray with a clatter and smiled at the girls. "I'm Evelyn Reid. Where do you ladies hail from?"

The lanky blonde with a swath of freckles on her face lifted her hand then pointed to the brunette beside her. "Nancy Barton, and this is my friend, Wanda Hilton. We're from Los Angeles, and we were lucky to be stationed together at Gardner. Now we're both here to get some more planes under our belts." Eyes wide, Nancy leaned forward. "The bandage on your forehead...are you the pilot who crashed yesterday?"

"Yes, but as you can see, I'm none the worse for wear." Evelyn sipped her coffee, and her lips twisted. Tepid and more bitter than usual. She set the mug on the table. "There will be an investigation as usual, but it should be open and shut. The engines failed, and I couldn't get them restarted. Frankly, I'm not impressed with the mechanics here."

"Really? Why don't they do something about that? You know, if we girls weren't up to snuff, we'd be booted out in a flash."

"It's not fair that we're treated differently." Wanda frowned. "When will these guys grow up and realize we're here to stay?"

Evelyn spooned vegetable soup into her mouth and swallowed. "Apparently, they think they can change our minds. Anyway, just be careful out there."

"What were you doing before you joined?" Nancy took a large bite from her sandwich.

"Crop dusting. I'm from Wisconsin."

"I did a bit of that, but then we opened a flight school for women." Nancy nodded. "Not too many places would take them as students. Lots of rich ladies, so I hated to give up the business, but it's important to do our bit for the war effort."

"Good for you." Evelyn reached for her coffee mug then pulled back. "You should be able to open up after the war, and with the number of hours you'll acquire by then, you'll be in demand."

"You think so?"

"Sure. Which planes are you here to learn?"

"The BT-13, P-39, and P-40." Wanda nibbled on a biscuit. "We've been ferrying bombers mostly. I'm looking forward to flying the smaller, more maneuverable planes."

"You'll love them. Not nearly as unwieldy as the bombers."

Nancy wiggled her eyebrows. "What I'm going to love is the gorgeous instructors and pilots. Have you seen these guys? Every one of them could be a movie star."

Wanda giggled and nodded. "You can say that again. I've already met a couple of dreamboats. Tall, dark, and handsome. Very Cary Grant."

"We're only allowed to look, you know. No dating allowed." Evelyn finished her soup and pushed away the bowl. "Besides, I don't have time for a relationship even if we were allowed to go out with these guys."

"Oh, honey. I'd make time." Nancy jerked her head toward a table of men near the window. "How do you choose from a collection like that?"

Evelyn pressed her lips together. These gals needed to focus on flying, not their love lives. Don't they realize how hard it is to be taken as a serious pilot? Prancing around and simpering, trying to grab the attention of the male pilots would ruin their credibility.

"You don't agree?" Nancy tilted her head.

"No, but I've been accused of being too determined and driven. You probably shouldn't listen to me. I'm not looking for a husband, so you're welcome to them."

"I don't want a husband either, but I wouldn't mind a good time to break up the monotony." She snickered. "All work and no play makes Nancy a dull girl."

"Wanda, too." Wanda laughed. "I've got navigation classes this afternoon. With any luck one of those hunky guys is leading the class. Seems like all my instructors at Sweetwater were old or bald or both."

Nancy rolled her eyes toward a group of men making their way across the mess hall. "My favorite is the rangy redhead. I've got a thing for ginger-haired men." She winked. "Totally swoonworthy."

Evelyn froze, her glass of milk gripped in her hand. Jasper. She hadn't seen him since the crash and had hoped to avoid him, but they both needed to eat, so running into him was bound to happen sooner or later. Why couldn't it be later? "That one's got quite an ego. You may want to give him wide berth."

"Oooh, there's a story behind those words. Some history perhaps?"

"He barked at me yesterday for not ditching the plane. Like the decision was his to make. Who does he think he is?" She set down her glass with a thunk. "Who yells at someone moments after they've survived a crash?"

"Wow, that's awful. Guess I'll have to find me a different redhead." Nancy wiped her mouth. "Well, I've yammered on long enough. I want to take a walk and clear my head before class. Nice to meet you, Evelyn."

Wanda rose. "See you around."

"Bye." Evelyn nodded in farewell as the girls picked up their trays and threaded through the tables. She peeked at the clock above the door. Ten minutes until instrumentation class. She had over five hundred hours of flight time, yet the army apparently didn't think her qualified on instruments. She'd breeze through and show them how wrong they were.

She dropped off her tray and hurried from the mess hall then broke into a jog. If she didn't hoof it, she'd be late to class, and then who would be ruining the WASP credibility?

Sunshine warmed her back, and she smiled. March in South Texas was nothing like Wisconsin. At home, she'd be hip deep in snow with no crops to dust. She was usually ready for spring well before her northern state lost its grip on winter.

Yanking open the steel door, she trotted through the corridor reading the numbers beside each classroom. One seventeen. She made it. Following a trio of women inside, she dropped into the first available seat, unfortunately front and center. She tucked her purse under the seat, brushed her hair from her eyes, and looked toward the instructor, who scribbled on the chalkboard.

She'd recognize the back of that head anywhere, but the man couldn't possibly be Jasper. He was a mechanic, and the army wouldn't tap him to teach class.

The instructor turned and sauntered to her. "Welcome to class, Miss Reid."

"Ja—I mean, Mr...uh..." Her gaze shot to his shoulder insignia. Captain? "Captain MacPherson. I don't understand. What are you doing here?"

He winked. "I'm your instructor. Didn't see that one coming, did you?"

Evelyn frowned. Apparently, he planned to embarrass her. "No. Since when does the army use their flight mechanics to teach instrumentation class?"

"They don't. I'm a pilot. Just like you."

"But—"

"But, as usual, you made assumptions based on almost no information." He surveyed the students. "Be advised that sort of behavior can get you killed." He turned back to her, his emerald gaze pinning her to the chair. "I'm a licensed pilot who flew my full share of missions across the pond, and now I'm here to teach you people."

She met his stare with one of her own. So much for avoiding him. Evelyn folded her hands and sent him a curt nod. She wouldn't spar with him in front of her classmates. It was going to be a long few days until she finished this course.

He walked to the chalkboard and began his lecture.

Evelyn sighed. Nancy was right. Jasper was one good-looking man. He'd been attractive in college, but in the years since she'd seen him, he'd grown more handsome. The angles on his face were more pronounced, and he walked with fluid confidence. Were his shoulders broader? How had that happened?

She blinked. Concentrate, girl. Flunking because you can't pay attention would be a disaster. Eyes glued to her notebook, she made copious notes. Perhaps if she didn't look at him, she could keep her focus on the subject matter. Not likely, but worth a try.

Forty minutes later, class ended, and she rubbed the back of her neck. Despite her knowledge about instrumentation, she had a lot to learn. This was not going to be the cakewalk she anticipated.

"Miss Reid, a moment." Jasper beckoned.

She waited until the room emptied then stood and gripped her notebook to her chest. That way he couldn't see her heart pounding. "Yes?"

"Look, I know this has all the makings of being an awkward situation, but I'll do my best to treat you with impartiality. You're a smart girl. You should be able to pass on your own merit."

Her eyebrow shot up. "Yes, I should, but it seems you're not as convinced. As long as you adhere to your promise to be unbiased, *awkward* won't enter the picture." She whirled and marched from the room. Same old Jasper. Sure he was smarter than everyone. Wonder who he'd annoyed to be relegated to teaching female pilots. Bet that stuck in his craw. She raked a hand through her hair. Would he do what he said, or would he fail her just because he could?

Chapter Three

Tiny whirlwinds of dust danced in the sunshine as Jasper hurried across the base. He shielded his eyes from the glare and squinted into the distance. He'd already checked three buildings for Evelyn to no avail. Was he imagining the idea that she was avoiding him? She arrived at class seconds before the door closed and nearly vaulted from her seat to be among the first to depart. She commandeered a seat in the back, answering questions when asked, but not volunteering information. Her demeanor was pleasant but distant.

He had only himself to blame. The moment he saw her in college ten years ago, he was enamored. Intelligent, gracious, and beautiful, Evelyn was everything he'd hoped for in a partner, a wife. Her excitement when she learned something new was palpable as she shared how she would implement the skills and knowledge to the company she planned to start. He'd encouraged her to soak up every scrap of information she could.

Without warning, his encouragement turned to detachment then criticism. Imperceptible at first then heavy-handed. He'd been young and stupid, jealous of her plans to strike out on her own as if she didn't need him. His fragile male ego shattered, he'd broken their relationship. Taking the coward's way out, he'd written a letter. With only four hundred students at the university, it had been a challenge to evade her, but he'd managed to remain out of sight. No wonder she hated him.

He owed her an apology, but she'd made it clear the day of the crash that she didn't want to discuss their failed relationship. Jasper pressed his lips together. She would not be happy with the news he had about the investigation.

A small oasis of picnic tables clustered under the calabash trees near the barracks. Jet-black hair glistened on a woman's head bent over a book. Finally. No one else had the blue-black tresses of a raven like Evelyn. His fingers itched to stroke her shining hair, but he'd lost that privilege too many years ago to count.

"Evelyn." He hurried forward.

She tucked a scrap of paper between the pages and closed the book. Irritation flitted across her face before she settled her features into an impassive stare. "Yes?"

Jasper gestured to the small volume. "Raymond Chandler. Still love a good mystery, eh?"

"I'm sure you didn't come to discuss my choices in reading material. What can I do for you?"

His heart clenched, and he licked his lips. "Uh, I've got the results of the inquiry into your crash, and I thought you'd want them." He handed her a sheaf of papers. "You can read the report, but the bottom line is that someone put sugar in the fuel tank. The amount was such that it took a while to do the dirty work of clogging the engine, which is why the motor didn't quit until you'd been in the air for a bit. This was sabotage, plain and simple."

"As I suspected. Good to be believed." Her hands tightened on the pages as she scanned the information. Her lips thinned to a slash, and her eyebrows nearly met above her nose as she frowned.

"Military police have been brought in for a full investigation. Whether the person intended to kill you or whoever took up the aircraft is moot. The incident is being considered attempted murder."

"What a mess." She handed him the file and slumped against the bench. "We just want to fly and do our bit for the war effort. Is that so hard to understand? To accept? We're doing the job to free up men for combat."

"And most guys are okay with that, but there are a few with medieval attitudes that your place is to keep the home fires burning." He reached to pat her arm then dropped his hand. No telling what she'd do if he touched her. "We'll get to the bottom of this, and I've been tasked with doing spot checks in the maintenance hangar."

"Meanwhile, there's a crackpot taking care of the planes for me and the gals. This has gotten personal, Jasper."

"I know, and I'll be praying we find the lunatic as soon as possible." At the word prayer, her eyebrow shot up, but she didn't comment. He folded the report and tucked the pages into his pocket. "You girls don't deserve this treatment."

"This base isn't the only place where we've run into problems. Last year, two WASP were killed at one of the North Carolina bases as a result of vandalism. And when the units first began to arrive there, the women weren't allowed in the cockpits. Ridiculous." She rubbed the back of her neck. "Do you know that the A-24s they were using for tow target training were worn out and not well-maintained because of the lack of parts? The first ten accidents at the camp were A-24s, and they happened over the course of less than ninety days. The powers that be tried to keep the information on the QT, but the gals talk among themselves. We know what's going on."

A chill swept over Jasper. "I wasn't aware of the incidents. No wonder you're suspicious."

"Now that there's evidence, you believe me. You couldn't take me at my word." Her hands gripped the book in her lap.

He blew out a loud breath. "You have every right to hate me, Evelyn, but I hope at some point you'll find room in your heart to forgive me. What I did...how I broke off our relationship was unconscionable. I was too immature to handle your love of anything else but me." He ran a hand over his crew cut. "But I've read your file. They provide information to instructors so we know the level of experience you bring to the table. Anyway, you did what you set out to do. Your crop dusting business was...is...a success, and you're certified on nearly twenty military aircraft. I can see why you were selected for pursuit plane training."

Her cheeks pinked, and a tiny smile tugged at the corner of her mouth.

"I'm sorry for hurting you, Evelyn." He risked taking her hand in his, and she didn't pull away. Hope flickered. "I don't expect you to accept my apology right away, but please consider being my friend. Nothing more. We were good together. We challenged each other and had fun. I miss that. Truth be told, I've yet to succeed in a relationship. I was engaged, but she dumped me." His mouth twisted. "That should make you happy."

"No." She withdrew her hand and crossed her arms. "For a long time, I wished you ill, but my anger was eating away at me, not you." A wry smile curved her lips. "What's the point? Anyway, I eventually got to a place where I didn't hate you quite so much. You're not entirely to blame. I was no angel. I didn't try to understand your point of view. To work things out when I saw you slipping away. I was too focused on my goals, so in that sense you were right. I loved my work more than I loved you. That wasn't fair."

"So...we can be friends?"

Evelyn shrugged. "I'm not sure I'm ready for that, Jasper, but I'll try not to be antagonistic."

"That's enough for me." His stomach rumbled, and he rose. "Apparently, I could use a bite to eat. How about you? Join me for lunch?"

"I'd like that." She tucked the book under her arm and walked beside him on the brick path toward the mess hall. Her heel caught between the pavers, and she stumbled against him.

Jasper's arms wrapped around her. "Careful!" She fit perfectly under his shoulder, like she had in college. The floral scent of her soap assaulted him, and memories of their ardent embraces crashed into his mind. He'd offered friendship, but did his heart want more?

Chapter Four

The minute hand on the clock above the classroom door inched forward. Evelyn's leg jiggled, and she tapped her pencil on the notebook on her desk. The gal next to her frowned, and Evelyn stilled. Would the lecture never be over?

"That's it for today, folks. Last session is tomorrow, so be prepared for some heavy-duty discussion." Jasper gestured to Evelyn. "Please remain."

Her heart skittered. What did he need to talk about? Was something wrong? Had he found the culprit who'd sugared her tank?

Students filed out, the buzz of conversation fading as the room emptied.

She rose and walked to the front of the room. "Do you have news?"

He shook his head. "Unfortunately, not about the vandalism, but I wanted to let you know you passed the written test for the BT, and I'm to be your check pilot."

Her eyebrow shot up, and she smoothed her features. Good thing she wasn't a poker player. Her face always said exactly what she was thinking.

"Is that a problem?"

"I'm not sure." Evelyn tapped her chin with her forefinger. "Did you ask for the assignment or was it the luck of the draw?"

"Would it bother you if I requested the duty?" He sighed. "I thought we'd come to a truce."

"We have; at least I think so." She shrugged. "Anyway, I'm concerned about your impartiality. We've got history. Can you put that behind you and not score me either too leniently or too harshly?"

"I'd like to think I can, but if you'd rather request another pilot, I'd understand."

She studied his face. He seemed to genuinely care about her comfort with the situation. His eyes held no guile, and the slight smile that curved his lips seemed sincere. She was making a mountain out of a molehill because her emotions were such a mess. Bad form. If she gave in to her feelings, she'd prove to those who'd ever made the argument that women couldn't be dispassionate and professional that they were right. "No need to make any changes. What time would you like to meet at the hangar?"

His smile bloomed, and his eyes crinkled at the edges.

Her breath hitched. So much for being detached.

He glanced at his watch. "I've got a phone call to make that can't wait, so how about thirty minutes?"

"Perfect. That will give me time to put on my flight suit." She pulled her books closer to her chest and headed out the door.

In the hallway, her barracks mate, Gladys Thorndike, leaned against the wall, a smirk on her face.

Evelyn squealed. "You startled me. Why'd you wait?"

"Being nosy. What did Captain Dreamboat want?

"To arrange for my check flight on the BT-13. Nothing exciting. Satisfied?"

"Absolutely." Gladys nudged her shoulder. "You'll get another plane on your list, so the possibility of more missions opens up. That's why we're here. But more importantly, you'll be trapped in a tiny compartment with one of the hunkiest instructors on the base. How lucky is that?"

"Hunkiest? Is that even a word?" She exited the building and hurried toward her home away from home, Gladys hot on her heels.

Gladys giggled. "It is now. Anyway, aren't you thrilled to be able to fly with him? He's one of the best. I heard he's got a chest full of medals and must have tons of stories. It doesn't hurt that he's so handsome."

Evelyn shook her head. "I didn't know about his awards. I'll see what I can find out from him during the flight. Makes me feel better about his qualifications."

"You were worried? I got stuck with Captain Quinn with my last check flight. He barely knows the difference between the rudder and the flaps."

"That can't be good. I haven't had him yet. Fingers crossed I never will." She stepped inside the barracks and ducked into her room. "As fun as this conversation is, I've got to change, and get over to the hangar."

"I'll expect a full report." Gladys winked and walked away, her laughter filling the hallway.

Evelyn rolled her eyes. That girl saw romance in every corner. She tossed her books on the cot and yanked open the tiny closet. She pulled out her flight suit and quickly changed her clothes. Running a brush through her hair, she inspected herself in the reflection, then pulled her locks into a ponytail. What was she doing? The flight was a test not a date. Focus, Evelyn.

She grabbed her jacket and scarf, took one last glance in the mirror, and left her cubby-sized room, slamming the door behind her. She raced out of the building and jogged across the base to the hangar. Sunlight warmed her back, and she blew out a deep breath, the tension in her shoulders melting away.

A beautiful day. A chance to fly. The job of a lifetime. She couldn't ask for more.

Jasper was waiting for her next to the plane.

Her stomach hollowed. Gladys was right. Jasper was one good-looking man. She lifted her hand in greeting, and he waved back, his emerald eyes sparkling in the afternoon rays.

He rubbed his hands together. "It's a perfect day to be in the air, so I've already done the visual on the exterior. Let's get to it, shall we?"

"Thanks. I was thinking the same thing about the weather on my way over." She slipped into her parachute and climbed into the front seat of the aircraft. Jasper took the seat behind her as she donned her headset. The tangy scent of his aftershave wafted toward her, and she swallowed then spoke into the mic, "Ready back there?"

"Roger." His warm voice rumbled in her ears.

"Okay." She licked her lips then began her preflight activities, trying to ignore the staccato rhythm of her heart. One by one, she reviewed each item on the checklist, and twenty minutes later she was satisfied with the craft's airworthiness. A spider of fear slithered up her spine. Had the fuel been tampered with or would today's flight be uneventful?

"Everything checks out, sir. Ready to begin taxi and takeoff."

"Roger that."

Evelyn started the engine and smiled. Nothing like the roar of an airplane motor. Sweeter than a Mozart concerto. "Control tower, this is four-four-three-one-four-two requesting permission for takeoff."

"Aircraft four-four-three-one-four-two, you are cleared for takeoff."

"Roger, control tower." She released the brake and advanced the throttle. The aircraft rolled forward, gradually gaining speed. She glanced at her instruments and nodded. All was well.

The engine choked.

Not again. She increased the throttle, but the motor continued to cough. Then it stalled. She gripped the yoke and braked, the aircraft coming to rest fifty yards down the taxiway. "Why does this keep happening to me?"

"Are you sure your preflight checks were up to snuff?"

"Yes." Evelyn spoke through gritted teeth. Nothing had changed. Jasper would never accept her as a capable, intelligent individual. "If you think I've messed up, let's switch places and you take over. See if you can get the engine going and the plane into the air. And after we're said and done, I'll be requesting another flight instructor because you're obviously biased against me."

Jasper blew out a sigh. He'd done it again. Put his size twelve into his mouth and offended Evelyn. When would he think before he spoke? "Look, I didn't mean—"

"Are you going to try to get this thing going or what?"

"No. Call the control tower, and explain we need help getting back to the hangar. We shouldn't take the plane up until it's been thoroughly checked, especially after your crash. There's no black smoke, but who's to say there aren't fuel issues again?"

"Fine." She picked up the mic and explained the situation.

"Stand by, aircraft four-four-three-one-four-two. We'll have you fixed up in a jiffy."

"Roger." Evelyn's voice was tight.

The silence in the cockpit was deafening, like the roar of an ocean. He searched his mind for a safe topic, but came up blank. He rubbed at a scratch on the side of the plane, his finger moving back and forth in the pacing motion his feet couldn't perform.

Several moments later, trucks and rescue vehicles raced toward them, dust billows swirling. They halted a short distance from the aircraft, and one of the men trotted to them and climbed onto the wing. He rapped on the canopy, and Evelyn slid open the glass. "Do you want us to drive her in?"

Evelyn shook her head. "No, I'll stay behind the wheel while you tow us."

The man nodded and jumped to the ground. Mechanics swarmed the airplane, and they soon had it hooked to a truck. With a lurch, the aircraft moved forward.

Jasper removed his headset and ran his palm over his crew cut. "Evelyn, please hear me out. You are an excellent pilot. From what I've seen, probably one of the best I know. You'd put many of my squadron mates to shame. I was stupid to question your abilities and your preflight actions. I'm sorry. Can we start over? Again."

Nothing.

He tried another tactic. "Can we at least agree I'm a heel?"

She snickered. "I'll grant you that."

"Thanks." He tugged at the collar of his flight suit. "When we get back to the hangar I'd like for you and I to do a complete inspection of every system with no help from any of the mechanics. I can't worry that we'll pick the wrong guy, and he'll cover his tracks."

"Is it possible that we have more than one culprit?"

A chill swept over him. "I hope not. That would be disastrous on too many levels to count."

"Okay. And Jasper?"

"Hmm?"

"I'm sorry I lost my temper."

"No problem, Evie." The nickname he'd used in college slipped out, unbidden. He cringed. Would she take exception to the endearment?

"Thanks."

He blew out a breath. Another tentative truce reached.

The aircraft came to a standstill, and the men quickly detached the towing harnesses. "You're all set, sir." The lanky crew chief saluted.

Jasper returned the salute and climbed from the cockpit. Evelyn scrambled out after him. She shed her parachute and laid it near the landing gear. He piled his chute next to hers. "Ready?"

A deep frown etched into her forehead, and she nodded.

Two hours later, they'd nearly completed their inspection. Jasper rotated his neck to ease the kinks that had formed from hunching over the engine. Nothing suspicious or out of whack. Perhaps the stall was a fluke. Evelyn would not be happy with that answer.

He glanced at her and smiled. Seemingly oblivious to her surroundings, she peered at one of the connectors, her tongue peeking out between her lips. A shining lock of ebony hair had come loose and dangled beside her cheek. He kneaded his hands to prevent tucking the hair behind her ear. Yeah, that would go over well.

Still the same girl. Concentration to the tiniest of details. There was no way she'd muffed the preflight activities. There must be something wrong with the plane. That was the only explanation.

Her wrench clanked, and she groaned then gestured at one of the parts. "Hey, look at this. I think we may have found the problem."

He pulled a flashlight from his pocket and focused the beam where she'd indicated. His eyebrows shot up. "Looks fishy to me, not like regular wear and tear." He poked the edges of the wires that had separated. "Looks like they've been filed just enough to come loose at some point. Whoever did this wants us to think they've been frayed, but the wires are too new. Good work."

She grinned, a triumphant gleam in her blue eyes.

He jumped to the ground. "I'll grab the maintenance log. Should tell us the last mechanic to work on this aircraft."

"True, but do you think whoever did the damage would actually sign his name?"

"Not necessarily, but if we talk to the most recent guy, he can tell us what sort of work was done on the plane. If inspecting the connectors wasn't part of the job, the vandalism could have occurred a while ago."

"True."

Jasper shuddered. This guy needed to be caught. Lives were at stake, his own included.

Chapter Five

"I've got to study, Gladys." Evelyn raked her fingers through her tangled hair. "I want to ace the final."

"Come on, Evelyn. Everyone's going to be there." Gladys stood in the doorway, hands on her hips. "Don't be a fuddy-duddy. You spend too much time in front of the books. A girl has to have fun now and again."

"I have fun."

Gladys rolled her eyes. "Outside of a cockpit."

"Oh. Well, to be honest, I'm not much of a dancer, so I'd just be taking up space in the officers' club."

"Nonsense. With the number of guys, you'll find plenty of partners to take you out on the floor. Think of it as doing your bit for the war effort and troop morale."

"Yeah, that's what it is." Evelyn grimaced. If only she knew whether Jasper would be there. Did she want him to be?

"Look, we haven't done anything since we got here, and I'm going to lose my mind. If you don't want to go for the boys, come as a favor to me. Admit it. You've got that stuff memorized already."

Evelyn's face heated. Why did it embarrass her to be so prepared? "All right. I'll go, but then you'll owe me one. Got that?"

Gladys squealed and executed a perfect fox-trot step. "Thank you. Now, put on your glad rags. The bus leaves in fifteen minutes."

"Fifteen minutes! That's cutting it close."

"I knew if you had too much time, you'd change your mind." Gladys stuck out her tongue then winked and slammed the door. "Wear your green dress and knock 'em dead." Her voice was muffled from the hallway.

Relieved she'd already showered, Evelyn raced around the room. She opened the wardrobe and yanked out her dress, slip, and heels. She tugged on the clothes, pinned up her hair, then applied her lipstick.

"Ready?" Gladys hollered from outside.

"Yes." Evelyn opened the door then went to the bureau and retrieved a lightweight sweater. Texas might be hot during the day, but sometimes the temperatures at night made her forget she was in the Lone Star State.

Gladys whistled and looped arms with her, tugging her toward the exit. "You look fantastic. The boys aren't going to know what hit 'em."

"I'm going for you, not the guys."

"Uh-huh. You'll change your mind once we're surrounded by those dreamy pilots and mechanics."

Outside the barracks, a cattle truck idled.

Evelyn's eyes widened. "We're going in *this*?"

"What a gas, right? One of the girls says the bases uses these converted cattle trucks all the time. It'll be fun. You can write home about the experience. Didn't you sign up to try new things?"

"No, I joined to fly."

"All aboard, ladies." One of the mechanics sat behind the wheel, a wide grin lighting up his face. "I promise not to hit every pothole in the road."

With a shrug, Evelyn followed the other women onto the truck and dropped into a seat next to Gladys. She nudged her barracks mate. "What else aren't you telling me? Punch will be served from a trough and food from a manger?"

"Funny. Just buckle up and hold on."

The truck bumped and swayed as it rolled down the macadam toward the officers' club. Open to all base personnel for the event, the building was sure to be mobbed. The vehicle passed groups of men and women walking or riding bicycles. Laughter and conversation surrounded Evelyn. She wrinkled her nose at the farmyard-tinged air within the truck. No amount of scrubbing would probably remove every vestige of cattle smell. The army was nothing if not creative.

After several minutes, they arrived at the club, and the bus emptied in a flash. Music filtered outside through the open windows of the club. The high-pitched giggles of women mingled with rumbling chuckles of men. Taking a deep breath, Evelyn stepped over the threshold and was enveloped in the writhing mass of people. Her high-heeled shoes gave her a bit more height than usual, but she was still shorter than the majority of people, so her view of the room consisted of backs and shoulders.

She poked Gladys and jerked her head toward the far wall. "I'm going to take a breather. Have fun."

"Already? We just got here."

"I know. This press is too much. I'll get the lay of the land from over there. I'm fine." Evelyn gave her a gentle push. "Go. Dance."

"Okay, but if I don't see you on the floor in the next ten minutes, I'm coming to get you."

"Deal."

Gladys threaded through the crowd and disappeared.

Evelyn blew out a deep breath and made her way to the wall. Leaning against the rough wood, she let her gaze rove the floor. The entire population must be in attendance.

"Hi. I see you found some calm in the chaos." A stocky man with a blond crew cut stood nearby, hands in his pockets. "I've seen you in the hangar. You're in pursuit training, aren't you?"

"Yes. Evelyn Reid from Green Bay."

"Cam Underhill, Minot, North Dakota."

"Another citizen from up north. How do you like Texas?"

"Too hot for my taste, and the temperatures have only begun to rise. I've been here since forty-two."

She nodded and continued to watch the swirling crowd. The guy seemed nice enough, but she wasn't ready to embarrass herself on the dance floor.

He moved closer, his gaze traveling from her shoes to the top of her head, then lingering on her figure. "You gals who fly are different than I thought you'd be."

Evelyn wrapped her arms around her middle and stepped back. She should have remained at the barracks to study. "How so?"

"Prettier. I figured you'd all be ugly and mannish. I mean, what woman in her right mind wants to pilot an airplane? That's not natural."

She pressed her lips together. Great. A roomful of people, and she was stuck with a misogynistic creep who gave her the willies. "To each their own, I always say." She moved farther away. Would he get the hint she wasn't interested in conversation?

"I don't understand why the army thinks it's okay to have women in the ranks. Bad idea, as far as I'm concerned."

Her anger flared. "We're here to help. There aren't enough male pilots, so the gals have been recruited to take up the slack." She frowned. "And we're doing a good job, so I guess you'll have to get used to us." Her gaze landed on a tall, lanky, red-haired man in a charcoal-colored suit, and her breath hitched. Jasper. And he looked good. Real good.

"You're too small to fly a plane." Cam had sidled his way to her side again. "You shouldn't be up there."

Skin crawling, she pulled the sweater in her arms close. She needed to get away from this weirdo. "Thanks for talking, but...uh...I'm going to find my friend. Have a nice night." Without waiting for an answer, she hugged the wall and made her way toward the front door. Air and quiet was what she needed.

She hurried outside and took a deep breath. A soft breeze lifted the tendrils of hair that had slipped from her pins. The tension melted from her shoulders. Sauntering away from the building, she cast an eye overhead. A clear night, the blue sky had deepened to sapphire, and pinpricks of light dotted the expanse.

Memories of stargazing with Dad tumbled forward, and she swallowed the lump that formed in her throat. What was he doing at the moment? What about Mom? The busyness of each day normally kept homesickness at bay, but the solitude and ridiculous conversation with Underhill had broken down her defenses.

Rubbing her forehead, she closed her eyes. Why did the men resent the women's presence? There was enough work to go around, especially with the shortage of male pilots. She should head back to the barracks. There was nothing for her here.

"A penny for your thoughts."

Evelyn whirled. "Jasper. What are you doing outside? All the fun is inside."

He cocked his head. "I could say the same to you."

"Yeah, well, I got talked into coming as moral support for Gladys. She's having a grand time without me. I'm thinking of turning in for the night."

"Surely, not. The evening is still young." He bowed. "Would you like to dance?"

Music wafted toward her. Did he remember that Ellington's "Three Little Words" was *their* song? She remained rooted in place.

His smile faltered. "Or not."

Her face heated. "I'm sorry. Of course, we can dance. You know how bad I am, so there won't be any surprises."

He beamed. "You were never as bad as you thought." He drew her into his arms, his hand warm on her hip through the thin fabric of her dress. His palm cradled hers, and tingles spread from her fingers to her shoulders. Her toes curled. How could he still affect her this way?

Jasper stifled a sigh. He'd be happy to stay in this place with Evelyn in his arms forever. His heart pounded, and his muscles quivered. The feel of her hand in his brought memories of the past surging into his head.

He moved in time with the music, their feet crunching against the dusty ground outside the club. Her eyes were wide, searching, questioning. He pressed her closer and tucked her head under his chin, losing himself in the song and the feel of her against his chest. Yes, he wouldn't mind if time stopped.

When they were like this, life seemed perfect. Then they interacted, and one or both ended up offended or upset. Why did he struggle with accepting her for the vivacious, intelligent woman that she was? Her smarts and sense of purpose were part of what drew him to her in the first place, then as time passed, he began to resent those very things.

What were the odds of them being thrown together again? Was it serendipitous or had God arranged their reunion? After all, He was known to have a sense of humor.

The song ended, but Evelyn didn't move away. He froze, his pulse hammering. Another piece started up, yet he didn't dance. What was he doing? He was letting the ambience of the night get to him...starry sky, rustling breeze, soft music, and a gorgeous woman in his arms.

He needed to get a handle on his emotions. He and Evelyn were the same people they used to be. Weren't they? He...they...could never go back to the way things were. He cleared his throat and released her then gestured to a bench not far from where they stood.

She nodded, and they sat.

He turned toward her and crossed his legs. "So...uh...what are your plans after you pass your next flight check?"

Disappointment clouded her eyes in the dim moonlight. "I'd like to learn to fly as many as possible, but I also need to get back to ferrying full time. I'd like to certify on the P-47 and P-51 then put in for an assignment. You?"

"I'll be here until the army moves me elsewhere. Training pilots." He blew out a breath. "Sometimes the work is tedious, but I saw enough death and destruction overseas. I lost too many friends."

"It must have been terrible." Her voice was low, melodic. "Were you frightened?"

"If I'm honest, sometimes. They try to train fear out of you, but..." He shook his head. "Will you go back to crop dusting? After winging your way in a P-51, a Piper Cub might be too tame for you."

She snickered. "You may be right. Some of the girls and I have talked about working for the airlines. As you've said, we'll have lots of experience with large aircraft and tons of miles racked up. Surely, the commercial airliners will need pilots with our knowledge and abilities."

Jasper swallowed a sigh. Did she realize how unrealistic her goal was? The army barely tolerated the women. He couldn't imagine the businessmen would feel much different.

"You didn't respond."

"I was trying to think of a polite way of letting you down."

She clenched her fists. "Why is it that guys can't stand to see us women succeed? To do things they can do? We're not trying to be men, but we want to be able to dream unfettered dreams. Not be chained to what their ideas of appropriate aspirations are."

He patted her hand. "This war has turned everything upside down. What we've known. What we've believed. Change comes hard."

"Are you patronizing me?"

"What? No. But I don't want to see you get hurt. Or frustrated." He ran his hand over his crew cut, a motion that was becoming a habit when he hung around Evelyn. "Have you considered other options?"

"You mean like air hostess or gate agent? No, thank you." Her eyes narrowed. "I'd rather not fly at all then take a job like either of those. That would be like asking you as an aeronautical engineer to be...I don't know...a draftsman...or whatever the engineering equivalent of that is." Her mouth twisted into a wry smile. "Or worse, teach women how to fly pursuit planes."

He chuckled. "You're right. I'm sorry. Old habits...uh...philosophies are difficult to set aside."

"We've only been back together a short time, and I've lost track of the number of times we've apologized to each other. When will it end?"

"We're still feeling our way. At least we're talking."

"True. I like it better when we don't fight."

"Me, too." And he liked it even better when they were dancing.

Chapter Six

The greasy aroma of fried chicken mingled with the buttery scent of mashed potatoes greeted Jasper as he entered the mess hall. His stomach rumbled in response. Up at dawn to finish reviewing his notes before class, he'd missed breakfast. He scanned the room. Was Evelyn here? He hadn't seen her in the two days since the party because she'd been tapped to make a ferrying run. Had she been able to find return transportation on an airliner or been stuck taking the long way home on a train?

Sunlight glinted on the raven-black hair of a woman with her back to him. Ah. She'd made it back. He realized he was grinning like a fool at her appearance and schooled his features into what he hoped was a more impassive expression. He hurried to the serving line and grabbed a tray. The two WASP in front of him were more intent on chatting then selecting their food, so he skirted them with a polite nod. After filling his tray, he pivoted to see if Evelyn was still seated.

Excellent. He weaved his way among the tables and slid into the vacant seat across from her. Despite the fatigue lines etched around her eyes, she beamed when she saw him.

He smiled. "You've been on the move. Good trip?"

She nodded. "Yes. I managed to bump a senator and catch a commercial flight within three hours of delivery. I had a layover in Chicago, but all in all, a great couple of days. Tired, though. If I nod off in class, don't give me any demerits."

He winked, and she flushed. "I promise. And if you'd rather skip and catch some shut-eye, I can cover the essentials later tonight, perhaps after dinner."

"That wouldn't be fair to the other girls who also do ferrying runs."

"I'd let them off, too, well, maybe." He nibbled on a chicken leg. "This is pretty tasty. Did we get a new cook?"

"I don't think so, but I could be wrong." She pierced him with her gaze. "Or maybe he's getting the hang of his job. Sometimes there's a learning curve."

He chuckled. "Point taken. Hey, rumor has it the base is getting some new planes."

Her eyes lit up, and she bolted upright. "Really? Do you know what kind? When are they arriving? Are they new releases? I've heard the aircraft companies are doing tons of research to put out better planes."

"Well, you're only a little excited about the prospect of new machinery."

Her face reddened, and she ducked her head. "Is it that obvious?"

Jasper raised his hand, forefinger and thumb held about an inch apart. Her joy was palpable...and adorable. "Just a smidge. As I said, just a rumor, so I don't have any of the skinny."

"You're an instructor. Don't they tell you when new inventory is arriving?"

Chewing the last of his chicken, he shook his head. "Nah, I'm too far down on the food chain to warrant any sort of explanation or information."

She pushed away her empty tray, her eyes glowing. "Gee, I'd love it if we got some new planes."

"What happened to putting in for an assignment after your P-47 and 51 certifications?"

"I guess I can't stay here forever just to learn every new toy that comes along." With a shrug, she grinned. "But a girl can dream."

Finished eating, he pointed to her tray. "Wanna go for a walk? There's still forty-five minutes until class, and I'm tired of being cooped up inside."

"Love to."

He collected her tray, carried it to the drop-off window, and led her out of the mess hall. An army air force captain didn't skip, but he sure felt like kicking up his heels. She'd agreed to go for a walk. In fact, she seemed to be enjoying his company. He stuffed his hands into his pockets so he didn't subconsciously reach for her hand. A move like that could be disastrous.

They strolled along the macadam, and he peeked at Evelyn. Arms swinging, she walked beside him, keeping up with his long strides. He shortened his pace. "Sorry. Wasn't thinking of your stubby, little legs."

She jabbed him with her elbow. "I'm doing okay."

"Yeah, is that why you're out of breath?"

"Ha! Not possible. I'm head of the calisthenics class."

"Of course you are." He rubbed his jaw. "I wanted to tell you that the investigation to figure out who is causing the mechanical problems isn't going well. I've questioned all of the staff, studied the logs, and performed spot inspections, but I've got nothing."

"Not surprising, but thanks for letting me know."

"I was hoping to have the situation tied up by now. Frustrating to be at square one."

"But as you said after the incident when we stalled, the culprit isn't going to log his sabotage hours."

"Too bad. That would be most helpful."

Evelyn giggled, and his heart swelled. Time with her always lifted his spirits. He gestured to the officers' club. "Say, it's awfully hot out here. Not sure what I was thinking by offering to talk a walk. How about if we play a round of pool before class." He made a show of looking at his watch. "Plenty of time for me to beat you."

"Not going to happen." She bounced on the balls of her feet. "You've met your match, Flyboy."

"You've improved since college? Sounds intriguing. Let's go." He held open the door, and she curtsied, a mocking smile on her face. Rising, she slipped past him, the tantalizing scent of flowers wafting from her hair. His pulse skittered, and he followed her inside.

She grabbed a cue from the rack then held up a nickel. "Heads or tails?"

"Ladies first."

"Great." She stuffed the coin into her pocket. "I won't turn you down." She bent, and in one quick motion, took her shot. The cue ball crashed into the pyramid of fifteen solid and striped balls, ricocheting them around the table. Several balls dropped into the pockets, and she laughed. "Stripes."

His jaw dropped. "Someone's been practicing."

She winked and took another shot.

Jasper prodded her leg with his cue stick then pulled back if he hadn't done anything.

"Hey!" She whirled. "Cheater."

"I waited until after you took your shot. You missed fair and square."

"Maybe." She gestured to the table. "See what you can do."

He studied the formation then moved toward her to take his shot.

She remained in place, a playful grin on her face.

"So that's how it's going to be." He pressed his shoulder against hers and shifted his weight, gently pushing her out of the way.

"You started it. And now you're cheating again."

"How's that?"

"By doing that I'm-bigger-than-you thing."

"I can't help it that you're a runt."

"This runt is going to beat you."

"Then let's make it interesting and place a wager on this *friendly* little game. If you win, you can cut the next two classes, and if I win...you have to go dancing with me again." His pulse quickened. How would she react?

"You're on. Guess I won't be seeing you in class." She stepped aside. "Table's all yours."

He took his shot, the green six-ball bouncing off the bumper and missing the pocket. Concentrate!

"Nice try." Evelyn chalked her cue stick then took a shot. The twelve ball sank followed by the fifteen ball. Two more shots, and she'd cleared the table of her set and the eight ball. She glanced at the clock above the door. "Looks like you have just enough time to make it to class. Think I'll head back to the barracks for a nap."

Jasper threw back his head and guffawed. "You are full of surprises, Miss Reid. Good thing we didn't have any money on the game, or I'd be short some serious cash. I knew you were competitive, but you seemed to have taken things up a notch."

She sent him a saucy smile. "If you think this is competitive, stay tuned."

"I look forward to it." Boy, did he.

Chapter Seven

Sunshine warmed the cockpit of the B-25, and Evelyn grinned at Gladys. This was the first time for her barracks mate to be her copilot, and the cross-country journey promised to be hours of laughter and chitchat. The weather had cooperated fully, giving her crisp visibility and gorgeous blue skies through which to soar.

She relaxed her grip on the yoke with a sigh. "There is nothing better than being in the air, don't you think?"

"Yeah, I could be up here forever." Gladys nodded and adjusted her headset. "Who needs to be tied down to a man when you can ride the thermals?"

"Don't you want to get married someday?" Evelyn raised her eyebrow. At twenty-three, Gladys was nearly ten years her junior, but by all accounts hadn't had a serious relationship. "Do you wants kids?"

"Nah. Most of the guys I've dated expect me to be the little woman at home. I'm a horrible cook, despise housekeeping, and the idea of raising children terrifies me. You're not married yet. What gives?"

Evelyn squirmed in her seat. Why had she taken the conversation in this direction? Jasper's face floated into her mind. "I'm not opposed to marriage, but I haven't found the right man." She frowned. "Although I am beginning to wonder if he's actually out there."

Gladys giggled. "And by that you mean, a guy who's willing to let you keep flying and run your business."

"I knew you'd understand." She glanced at Gladys. "How about if you take the wheel for a bit."

"Love to." Gladys grabbed the yoke. "Did you ever think you'd be flying for the military? Sometimes I wake up and have to pinch myself for my good luck."

"Not in a million years, but your being here has nothing to do with luck. You're a great pilot. You've worked hard to pass the classes and rack up the hours. I didn't see you struggle with any of the subjects. Math about kills me."

"Believe me, there are areas that are tough for me, but I try not to show it." She blew out a deep breath. "I was stunned when Hilda washed out. I was sure she was going to ace her check flight, but she tanked. Rumor has it she froze at the wheel, and the instructor had to bring in the plane."

"I think something else was going on with her. A couple of days before the flight, I found her crying over a letter from home. She wouldn't tell me what it said and got angry when I pressed her, so I wonder if she received bad news."

"Or got a Dear Jane. Since I've been in the WASP, more than a few of the gals were the recipients of those awful missives." Gladys twisted her mouth. "Dear So and So, I'm sorry to do this in writing, but I don't love you anymore because blah, blah, blah."

"Could be. She was pretty upset."

"You know who surprised me was Olive. She's such a timid thing. I couldn't believe she'd made it through the regular program and got selected for pursuit training then streaked to the top of every class."

"True, but she's smart as a whip and follows every procedure to the tiniest detail. And her memory is incredible. She helped me memorize terms during military law class."

"Nice. She was only in my navigation class, so I didn't get to know her too well. We'll have to pal around when we get back."

The aircraft bucked, and Evelyn's stomach flipped.

Gladys gasped and grasped the yoke with both hands. "Oops. Guess I got too complacent. Sorry."

Evelyn giggled. "You're going to lose your flying privileges, young lady."

"No matter how many times I hit turbulence, I never get used to the feeling. My whole life flashes before my eyes."

"Really?"

"No, but it does get my heart racing." She tilted her head. "All kidding aside, what we do is dangerous, especially when we have to ferry a plane from the factory that's never been tested or take an aircraft to the boneyard. Who knows how many things are wrong with the old bird? Do you ever think about dying?"

"Sometimes, but I know where I'm going after this life." Evelyn's pulse raced. Would Gladys want to hear about God or be offended? Faith could be a hard topic for some people.

"You believe in God?"

Evelyn nodded. "Do you?"

"No, but I've been to church a few times. Mostly, Christmas time. I have a friend who is a believer. She's talked to me about it a little bit, but...I don't know...seems too good to be true."

"I understand, but it's not. God loves us with no strings attached. He wants a relationship with us and sent His Son, Jesus, to make that happen. When we believe in his resurrection, we become part of God's family. He's our heavenly Father."

"The father part is what I struggle with. My own father...well...let's just say there isn't anything heavenly about him."

"I'm sorry you've had a difficult family life. A situation like that makes it hard to relate, doesn't it?"

"Yeah. When my dad was sober, he wasn't too bad. Not lovey dovey, but at least he didn't hit us. Unfortunately, the good times were few and far between." Gladys shook her head. "Seems like life's been pretty good to you. Must be easy to have faith."

"Appearances can be deceiving." Evelyn swallowed the lump that formed in her throat. "I lost a younger sister in a car accident while I was in high school. Not that it compares, but getting dumped from a serious relationship during college was also painful. I thought he was going to propose. Instead, I got a Dear Jane."

"Oh, Evelyn, I had no idea." Gladys turned toward her. "Shame on me for making assumptions."

"That's okay." Evelyn patted her shoulder. "But I want you to know that even though I still hurt from these events, God got me through them. I'm far from hunky dory some days, but He gives me a peace that I can't explain or understand. You could have it, too."

"I'll think about it." She sighed. "I'm sorry to hear about your breakup. No wonder you're off guys, although some of these pilots might make you change your mind. I mean, don't you feel even a little bit of a thrill when you're in the air with that dreamboat Captain MacPherson?"

"Uh...he's actually the one who ditched me."

Gladys's jaw dropped, and her mouth formed a perfect O. "Well, I be a monkey's aunt. You two have played it cool. I had no idea about your...uh...history. Did you know he was going to be here before you arrived?"

Evelyn shook her head. "No, and the first time I saw him was the morning of my crash. He's one of the people who showed up after I hit the ground. To say I was stunned is an understatement."

"Do you think you'd ever get back together? I know he hurt you, but do you have any residual feelings for him? He certainly makes my heart pound whenever I see him."

"He's all yours, Gladys. I can't imagine ever having a relationship with him again." If only, she could convince her heart.

Jasper sighed and shifted in the back seat of the BT-13. This check flight was his second of the day and didn't promise to be any better than the first. A gorgeous day to be in the air; the skies were cloudless and the winds nonexistent. But his student pilot seemed more interested in flirting than flying. "Please execute a stall and recovery."

"Okay. I guess a highly skilled flyer such as yourself gets bored teaching us young gals. Although I'm not too young." She giggled. "You must have been very brave during your time in combat."

"No chitchat, Miss Franklin. We're here to determine if I can certify you in the Vultee, not discuss my personal life or yours."

"Sorry." Her head swiveled as she surveyed her surroundings then reduced the aircraft's speed. A bit of buffeting as the nose pitched forward and the plane began to lose altitude.

He checked his watch as the seconds passed.

She lowered the nose to decrease the angle of attack which increased their air speed. Moments later, airflow over the wings was restored, and the plane's trajectory smoothed.

"Well done. Please repeat the action twice more then circle the base."

"Yes, sir." She performed the required tasks then flew toward the collection of buildings. "You know, a bunch of us go out sometimes on the nights we're off. Do the instructors get time off? It would be fun to pal around, wouldn't it?"

Jasper gritted his teeth. Could she not remember he'd asked her not to talk, and did she not care, or did she simply have no control? "Miss Franklin, what did I say about prattling on?"

"Oops. I'm a chatterbox. My mother has always said my mouth will get me in trouble, and she was right. I can't tell you the number of times I had to go to the principal because I wouldn't stop talking in class."

"You're—"

"Sorry, sorry. I'm shutting up now. Really."

He shook his head. Even her apology was long winded. Did she think that by flirting with him, she had a better chance of receiving her certification? Was she trying to use her feminine wiles to get in good with him? There was a strict rule about the WASP dating the instructors, but it happened. Some of the higher-ups thought a female pilot program was wrong, and her behavior would do nothing to endear her to them.

Polly was a good pilot. She didn't need to carry on to get his approval. Should he say something about her behavior, or would his comments hurt her feelings? He might not be the warmest guy around, but he didn't intentionally make people feel bad. That's what he'd tried to tell Evelyn when he first saw her after ten years.

Evelyn.

His heart rate increased, and he blinked. She wasn't even in the cockpit, and she affected him. Was she doing all right on her cross-country trek? Gladys was also a good pilot and would serve as an excellent copilot. The weather report for their journey was smooth sailing for the entire trip, so they should be fine. Then why did he worry when he thought of her flying that big bird over four hundred miles?

"Something wrong, Captain?"

"What? No. Why do you ask?"

"I've asked you three times if I'm supposed to continue circling or do you have another skill you'd like to test? Could you at least pretend to pay attention?"

His face heated. "Sorry, Miss Franklin." He could definitely do without the drama and machinations associated with instructing the female pilots. A male pilot wouldn't be put out because he wasn't hanging on to her every word or movement. "Head back to base. We're done."

"Something...or someone on your mind, sir?"

"Nothing you need to concern yourself with. Just keep your eyes on the sky and your instrument panel." He blew out a breath. And he'd try to keep his eyes on his job rather than a certain beguiling student pilot from his past.

Chapter Eight

Humidity clung to the air like a cloak, and Evelyn blew out a deep breath. Her back ached from sitting on the wooden bench waiting for the train. Gladys sat beside her, nose buried in an Armed Services Edition of Graham Greene's *The Ministry of Fear*. Typically shipped overseas, a few of the ASEs had found their way to the stateside bases. One of the boys had told her the pocket-sized paperbacks were almost as popular as the pinup posters. Almost, but not quite.

She should have picked up a newspaper or magazine, but she was sick of reading casualty lists even though the war was starting to turn in favor of the Allies. With her eyes focused elsewhere, she wouldn't have to see the disdainful glances from members of the public who didn't understand why women walked around in pants. Despite press about the program, many people hadn't heard of the WASP.

Last night's debacle at the restaurant had been a prime example. The maître d' had refused to serve Gladys and her, giving them an icy how-dare-you-enter glare and stating, in no uncertain terms, that the establishment didn't serve women wearing slacks. After a long day of flying, she was starving and in no mood to put up with his derision, so she'd whipped out her identification card and demanded to see the manager. The man barely seemed convinced, but he let them in, nonetheless.

Voices echoed in the cavernous station, and footsteps vibrated the platform. Evelyn glanced at the massive clock on the wall for the umpteenth time. Only minutes since she'd last checked.

"Stop fidgeting." Gladys poked her with her elbow. She pulled out another ASE volume. "Here."

Evelyn grabbed the book and flipped it over. "*Love at First Flight.* Clever. What's it about?"

"A pilot in training. Supposed to be funny."

"Hmm. Depends. Could be too close to the truth."

"There are clever illustrations." Gladys shrugged. "Beats watching the clock and scowling at the other travelers."

"I'm not—"

"Yes, you are."

"Okay, fine. I'll read."

The distant rumble of the train filtered into the station, and Evelyn tucked the book into her pocket. "Guess I'll wait until we're on our way." She rotated her neck. "I do love ferrying the planes, but getting back to base is tedious."

With a roar and squealing brakes, the locomotive clattered to a stop. They pushed to their feet and waited for the sea of disembarking passengers to clear. Conversation and laughter mingled with crying babies and shouts from the porters.

Evelyn linked arms with Gladys and followed the surge of people jostling their way onto the train. Stretching on her toes, Evelyn tried to see if there were any vacant seats. Gladys tugged her to the right, and they inched toward the rear of the car. About two-thirds back, a pair of army majors sat, heads together, pointing at something on a piece of paper. One of them glanced up and frowned. He jabbed his seatmate, who looked up. The man's eyebrows shot up and nearly disappeared in his hairline.

He rose and held up his hand. "Who are you, and why are you wearing those uniforms?"

"We're with the Women Air Service Pilot organization and are headed back to our base in Brownsville." She swallowed a sigh and fumbled in her purse for her ID card. So much for the rest of their journey going smoothly. These men were in the army. How could they not know about the WASP?

Gladys handed the man her card and beamed. "Just doing our bit for the war efforts, sirs. We ferry planes and tow targets, among other activities."

The man snatched their identification and peered at them for a long moment then gave them to his traveling companion. "Have you heard of this group? Sounds fishy to me."

"Yeah, we got some memorandum about it a few months ago, but I've never seen any of them. Guess they're on the up and up." His gaze raked their figures. "Although why their uniforms are comprised of pants, beats me. Totally unfeminine."

Evelyn pressed her lips together to keep from blurting out anything that would get her gigged from the program. Instead, she pinned on a smile and waited for the men to finish insulting her and Gladys. Would this trip never end?

He finally returned their cards and sat down without another word.

"We're dismissed, sir?"

He shrugged and waved his hand toward the back of the car.

Her chest tight, Evelyn continued down the aisle. Her nostrils flared, and she nibbled her lower lip. She couldn't arrive at the base soon enough.

The last row in the car held two empty seats, and she dropped into the one beside Gladys whose red face told of her own anger at the cavalier treatment by the officers.

Evelyn patted Gladys's arm. "I'm going to try to sleep. Wake me when we get there."

"Can you take time to pray that something diabolical happens to those men?"

Stifling a giggle, Evelyn shook her head. "That's not the way prayer works. Instead, I'll ask God to help me get over my anger at those two galoots."

Gladys's eyes widened. "What? After they were so awful? Why would you do that?"

"Two reasons: they don't know or care that I'm angry, so the emotion is useless in that regard, and if I let my anger fester, it's detrimental to me and anyone I come in contact with."

"I don't understand how you can be this way. I'm so mad I want to slap those guys. That's why I can never be a believer. I'm not good enough."

"Oh, honey. None of us is. That's why we need God. He keeps us from messing up. And as tempting as it is to take out my hurt and upset on those men, doing so would exacerbate the situation, and no one would win."

The door closed with a thud, and the train lurched forward in a cloud of coal-smelling smoke. Wood creaking, the passenger car swayed and bumped along the tracks. Clickety-clack. Clickety-clack.

"Thanks for being such a good friend, Evelyn." Gladys gave her a tremulous smile. "I'm learning a lot from you. I'm not ready to get on board with this God thing, but I respect what He's done for you."

"Anytime you want to talk about Him—"

"I know." She pointed out the window at the landscape that raced past. "Texas scenery is nothing like where I'm from, but it sure is pretty in a stark kind of way."

Evelyn nodded. Apparently, Gladys was done with deep, personal discussions. Perhaps that was best. Hopefully, the four hours or so it would take them would be long enough to dissipate Evelyn's anger at the army officers. God had His work cut out for Himself.

Alternately praying and dozing, she arrived at the Brownsville station stiff and sore, but feeling less antagonistic. She'd try to maintain her composure for her and Gladys's sake. They caught a bus to the base, checked in, then went to their barracks.

Gladys tossed her bag on the floor and flopped onto her bed. "I'm not on the schedule for another two days, so I'm going to curl up and finish my book." She rubbed her eyes. "Or take a nap. Sleeping on the train isn't exactly restful."

"Have fun. As exhausted as I am, I'm a bit keyed up, so I'm going to head to the hangar and see if we've gotten any new aircraft. I thought we had some birds scheduled to arrive while we were away." Evelyn closed the door to Gladys's room, ducked into hers, and unpacked her bag. Grabbing a set of fresh clothes, she tucked them into the luggage and set it in the bottom of the wardrobe. She finger-combed her hair. Ready to go at a moment's notice.

She left the barracks and strolled the path that led to the hangar. Yes, she was tired, but being around the aircraft rejuvenated her. The frustration of the last thirty-six hours began to seep from her shoulders as she approached the cavernous building. Planes were her best friend. They did what they were told unless there was a maintenance issue, but that was repairable. People weren't as easy to fix.

Her feet slapped against the concrete floor and she approached a P-39. Its silver bullet-shaped body gleamed in the dappled sunlight. She reached up and stroked the wing, the metal cold against her fingers.

"Hey, Evelyn."

She jumped and whirled around.

One of the mechanics stood about three feet away. Arnold...Alvin...Adam? What was the man's name? More importantly, how did he get so close without her hearing him? "Uh..hi."

"Whatcha doin'?"

"Out for a walk and thought I'd visit. Just got back from a run and needed to stretch my legs."

He moved closer. "And you came to see me?"

She licked her lips. "No, the planes. Did we get any new ones?"

"I'm glad you came. I've been wanting to speak to you." He stepped forward and stroked her arm.

The hair on the back of her neck prickled, and her skin crawled. Where were the other mechanics? Trapped between him and the landing gear, she had nowhere to move. She made a show of looking at her watch. "What did you want to talk about? I don't have a lot of time. I...uh...have somewhere to go."

His eyes narrowed, and he gripped her shoulder, his fingers biting into the muscle.

She winced. "You're hurting me."

"And you're trying to put me off. All you pilots are the same. You think you're better than us. We're the ones that keep your planes in working order." He pressed himself against her. His hot breath brushing her cheek. "We have the power to keep them in the air. You need us, yet you treat us like we don't matter." An ugly laugh vibrated his chest. "But it's up to us whether you live or die."

Her heart pounded, and she struggled, but his grip remained firm. His body, large and unmoving, blocked her escape. "Please, let me go. We can talk, but not like this."

"No. You missed your opportunity. Now, we'll talk without words." He bent his head and pressed his lips to hers, rough and hard.

She whimpered and tried to shove him away to no avail. Her heart pounded in her ears. *God, please save me.*

Then, suddenly, he was gone.

"Alex, get your hands off her, you brute."

Evelyn sagged against the upright on the landing gear and gaped at Jasper.

Jasper twisted the mechanic's arms behind his back then pushed him toward the wall. "What do you think you're doing?"

"She was asking to be kissed."

"I doubt that, and I have half a mind to knock your block off for taking liberties with her. As it is, I'll see to it that you're court-martialed."

"You can't do that."

"Maybe not, but I know people who can."

"Hey—"

"Enough. We're going to get the MPs down here to sort out this mess."

Evelyn touched her bruised and swollen lips. A wave of nausea rolled over her, and she put her head between her knees to keep from retching. Her vision swirled. If Jasper hadn't come...*Thank you, God, for sending Jasper.*

Her hero. Whether she wanted him to be or not.

Chapter Nine

Arms crossed, Evelyn sat beside Jasper in the CO's office. They had followed the jeep carrying two MPs and Corporal Alex Vance from the hangar. The commanding officer looked alternately irritated and appalled. Jasper's expression was impassive, but the muscle jumping in his jaw told her of his suppressed rage.

Perspiration trickled between her shoulder blades, and nausea still roiled in her gut when she looked at her attacker. She wiped her damp palms on her pants. So much for getting rested and rejuvenated after her trip. Wait until Gladys heard what happened.

Looking down his nose at her and Jasper, Commander Lynch frowned. "I'll expect a full written report, but needless to say, the intervention by MPs requires me to address this incident immediately. I've heard your sides of the story, and considering that the corporal here has been less than cooperative, additional investigation will be necessary."

"Sir, I'd like to add a few words." Jasper raised his hand. "About Miss Reid."

"I wasn't quite finished, MacPherson, but if you think the information you have is important enough to interrupt me, go ahead."

Jasper's face reddened to his hairline. "Well, I wanted to provide a character reference for her. She is a graduate of the second class of WAFS and has continued on with the WASP, racking up hundreds of hours of flying time. Her skill at handling the pursuit planes is exemplary; she certifies more quickly than any student I've ever had. Her record is spotless, and she has proven herself a leader among the other pilots. She's an asset to the army air force, and we are lucky to have her on our team."

Evelyn's eyes widened. When had Jasper's opinion changed about female pilots and the WASP program? And to be effusive about her skills and background was surprising.

"What does this have to do with the current situation?"

"Uh...well, she has no reason to make up the accusations, as Corporal Vance has indicated. He accosted her without provocation."

"However, you don't know that for certain. You didn't witness the event."

"No, sir. But—"

"That's enough, Captain. I appreciate your input, but it has little bearing on our conversation."

"One more thing, sir."

Commander Lynch blew out a loud breath. "What is it now, MacPherson? This had better be good."

"I'd like to question the corporal about the part he played in the incidents of sabotage we've experienced over the last few weeks."

"What sabotage? I didn't do anything to the planes." Corporal Vance shook his fist, spittle flying from his mouth.

"How did you know I was talking about planes if you had nothing to do with the events?"

"What else could you mean," Corporal Vance sneered. "Besides, I heard the other mechanics talking about what happened. Secrets have a way of getting out on a base this size."

Jasper rubbed the back of his neck. "I'm not convinced, and I believe we should include that possibility as part of the investigation."

"Telling me how to run my outfit, MacPherson?" The commander pursed his lips.

"No, sir. But Ev—I mean, Miss Reid has been victimized twice. First, the sugar in her gas tank, and now this personal attack."

"Look, I do the job to the best of my ability. I take pride in my work." The corporal held out his hands. "Maybe I got a little...uh...inappropriate with the lady, but I got mad. Her and the others shouldn't be here. It's not natural them trying to do a man's job. They need to stay home...do women's stuff. But I didn't do nuthin' to her plane or anyone else's. I swear on my mother's grave." He looked mulish. "And I'm not the only one who thinks the women need to go."

Evelyn shuddered. Who else thought the WASP shouldn't be flying? Could there be more than one saboteur? Did the girls have a chance of being successful with men trying to undermine them, or worse, take them out of the picture completely by whatever means necessary?

"I don't care what you think, Corporal." Commander Lynch pointed at him. "You're not paid to have an opinion. You're here to keep my planes in the air. Got that?"

"Yes, sir."

"Now, having said that, I believe you need some time to consider your actions and a night in the brig is the place to do that. I'll take the evening to determine my course of action." The CO swung his piercing gaze at her and Jasper. "And you two, get those reports written immediately. I want them on my desk in thirty minutes. Then I've got a special assignment for you, MacPherson. Apparently, some of the men on this base don't understand their expected behavior with regard to the WASP. The women are here. We have to live with it. You're to call together the entire base and explain the situation. The men are to remain professional at all times and allow the women to do their jobs without interference."

"Wouldn't this be better coming from you, sir?"

"I've got a war to run, MacPherson. You seem rather...uh...passionate about the subject. You handle it. Clear?"

"Crystal, sir."

"Good. Dismissed."

The MPs nudged the corporal, and they marched out the door.

Evelyn saluted then licked her lips and followed Jasper. Her heart pounded, and the nausea continued to roll over her. What a day. All she'd wanted to do was spend some time with the planes and regain her equilibrium. Instead, she was more agitated than when she'd arrived back on base.

She glanced at Jasper. His opinions might differ from hers, but that didn't change the fact that he was a good man. Fair and just, wanting to see people get their fair shake. His speech about her and the WASP program was eloquent, but the CO didn't care. What had he said? "They're here. We have to live with it." She blew out a breath. Why did life have to be such a struggle?

The early afternoon sun beat down on Jasper's head. He was already overheated as a result of the discussions in the CO's office. A debacle. "They're here. We'll have to live with it." The man needed to respect all his pilots, not just the men. And to pawn off the all hands to Jasper was the coward's way out.

He pressed his lips together and peeked at Evelyn. Exhaustion etched lines on her ashen face. She also looked a bit green around the gills, to coin a phrase.

"Where would you like to set up camp to write our reports?"

She shrugged, her eyes clouded and downcast.

Where was the spunky, take-no-prisoners woman he knew? He bumped her shoulder. "So that didn't go as well as I'd hoped, but we'll get to the bottom of this. I promise. Especially, now that the MPs are involved. Before, it was only me nosing around. They're professionals."

"True." She rubbed her forehead. "Perhaps it's fatigue talking, but the lack of support from the CO was discouraging. The meeting felt like he was simply going through the motions. Doesn't seem fair. If a man had been attacked in some way, would Commander Lynch take him more seriously?"

"Let's head to the mess hall. We can grab a drink of some sort." He cocked his head. "When's the last time you had something to eat?"

"Last night."

"We're definitely going to the mess hall to get you fed, missy." His heart tugged at her wan appearance. "Can't have you wasting away."

They made their way across the base and entered the squatty building that held the dining room. Despite the open windows, the air was warm and stifling.

"Hmm, other than the lack of sun, this place isn't much better than outside." He led her to the serving area. "I'm not sure I'll ever get used to this Texas heat."

"Me, neither." She picked up a tray and scooted along the line.

"You actually have to select food." He tugged her tray to the beginning of the line and nodded to the man behind the table. "Two chicken sandwiches, please. And some of those green beans."

"Jasper—"

"No argument." He winked at her, and her face pinked. At least he was getting a response. Her lethargy concerned him. At the end of the line, he picked up a couple of oatmeal raisin cookies then gestured toward a nearby table.

Evelyn set down her tray then lowered herself into the chair, staring at the food in front of her. Finally, she picked up the sandwich and nibbled a corner.

He smiled. Excellent. She was eating. He sat across from her and took a bite from the cookie.

She swallowed, her eyes wide. "Since when do you eat dessert first, Mr. By-the-Book?"

"Got your attention, didn't I?" He patted her arm. "Listen, I know the last thirty-six hours have been dreadful, but hang in there. You're a strong woman, and no matter what happens, I'm behind you. The WASP gals have worked like yeomen to support the air force. You all should be proud of what you've done."

Picking up her glass, she rubbed at the condensation on the side then gulped the amber liquid. "Thanks for what you said in there. I didn't know you felt that way about us...and me. I appreciate your support." She put down her glass with a tired smile and squeezed his fingers.

Tingles shot up his arm. His chest swelled. Truth be told, he'd been glad to stick up for her and the girls. It was about time someone did. "I'm sorry that the CO acted like he did, but I guess he's looking at the big picture...the war. We don't know what he's dealing with, so our problem may seem infinitesimal."

"I don't understand how an attack on one of his staff is insignificant. He needs us to do our job to support the war effort. That should mean something."

"I agree, but we've got to meet people where they are." He shrugged. "Even if we don't like their...uh...location."

A thoughtful look on her face, she chewed on her sandwich. After several moments, she sighed. "Thanks for the reminder. Guess I need to look at him and the corporal through God's eyes, which is hard."

"No kidding. I wanted to give in to my anger and wallop that guy good. Make him think twice about accosting a woman ever again. But then I'd be no better than him, to say nothing of a trip to the brig myself."

She pushed away her tray. "And thanks for making me eat." She gestured to the small pile of beans and half sandwich. "With rationing, I feel like I should finish everything, but I'm stuffed."

He grinned and grabbed her sandwich. "The food won't go to waste. Fork over those beans."

She scooped the vegetables onto his tray then sat back, her gaze surveying the room behind him.

"You should grab some shut-eye, but in all the hullabaloo I failed to share my good news...the reason I came looking for you. We've got a pair of P-51s coming in next week, and you've been tapped to be one of the first to get hours in them."

A smile lit her face, and she bolted upright, all traces of fatigue gone. "You wouldn't tease a girl, would you? I've been dying to get a chance at those babies."

He chuckled. "I'm not joking. And if you make it worth my while, I'll put you on the schedule ahead of everyone."

She raised her eyebrow. "Yes?"

"Have dinner with me tomorrow night. Just the two of us."

Her smile widened, and she nodded.

His chest lightened. He could get used to seeing her look at him like he'd just hung the moon and stars for her.

Chapter Ten

Evelyn rubbed her hands together as she sat in the cockpit of the P-51. Jasper perched on the wing and looked over her shoulder. His woody aftershave tinged with sweetness enveloped her in the cramped space. She blinked and tried to focus on the instrument panel. The single-seat aircraft didn't allow room for a copilot, so he would not be able to go into the air with her. Instead, they would spend several hours reviewing the plane's layout, capabilities, and nuances.

The idea of soloing without airtime with him beside her nearly paralyzed her. What if she forgot what he told her? What if she got confused? What if something unexpected happened? Would she live to tell the tale?

Her pulse raced. Sleek and powerful, this version had a two stage, supercharged Merlin engine that was heavier than the original Allison and pushed the center of gravity forward. Would she be able to handle the magnificent plane?

"You can do this," Jasper's voice rumbled. "Take a deep breath. We'll take all the time you need to become familiar with the aircraft. Remember, you wanted to fly her."

"Seemed like a good idea at the time." Her laugh sounded nervous in her ears. He'd think her a ninny, and more important, perhaps wonder if she was up to the task. She cleared her throat and nodded. "Yes, and I still want to. But at more than fifty thousand dollars, I'm a bit nervous about taking the old gal up."

He tugged on her ponytail, and gooseflesh raised on her arms. "I repeat: you can do this."

Evelyn straightened her spine. Yes, she could. Last week's attack and the commander's attitude had done a number on her confidence. The MPs seemed no closer to discovering the identity of the culprit, but she was alive, unharmed, and flying in the chance of a lifetime. "The manual promises more maneuverability."

"You won't believe what a sweet ride this machine provides. When I went up the day after this one arrived, it felt like she was reading my thoughts. This craft will be able to go nose to nose with any fighter out there. I didn't get one when I was flying sorties. Would have been nice."

"They can escort the bombers all the way to Berlin and back, can't they?"

"Yes, ma'am. They'll soar to forty thousand feet. The more of you gals who can certify, the better. We need to get these planes in the boys' hands."

Evelyn nibbled her lower lip. How long would the WASP continue to ferry? "One of the girls came back from Wichita last night and said rumors are swirling that we're going to be disbanded."

"What? I thought Congress was considering making you part of the military."

She shrugged and rubbed at a spot on the instrument panel. "Maybe."

He grabbed her hands and put them on the yoke. "Okay, enough talking about the higher-ups. Who knows what they're doing? But for now, we're flying one of the best aircraft on the planet."

"Well, not flying yet..."

He chuckled and poked her side.

Twisting away from his fingers, she giggled. "Be serious."

"Why?" He continued to poke her side. "You're trapped, and I plan to take advantage of the situation. I happen to know you are very ticklish."

She laughed and shrieked until she was breathless. "I'm going to write a report on you, mister."

"Right. You wouldn't dare." He winked. "Now, pay attention while I cover some of the differences in this plane from the others you've been flying."

Her pulse sped up. The sun glittered on his ginger-colored hair, and his eyes crinkled on the sides as he smiled. The girls would be jealous on two counts: her assignment on the P-51 and the handsome instructor.

What would life have been like if she'd given up her dream to own a crop dusting business and fly for a living to marry Jasper? Would their marriage be a strong partnership, or would she have resented her choice to stay home and raise a family?

She listened as he outlined the procedures for the heavier plane. Only a few differences, subtle but important. Tearing across the sky at almost four hundred and fifty miles an hour would be like nothing she'd ever experienced. The journey would be sweeter with Jasper beside or behind her, but that wasn't an option in most of the pursuit planes.

He covered a few more of the basics, and she nodded, confidence growing as she understood most of what he told her.

The P-51 was the last plane she was scheduled to learn before getting her next assignment. Where would the army send her? California would be nice. Sunny and warm, although every trip would be a long one if she lived there. Perhaps Wichita made sense. She could ferry the new planes right out of the factory.

Her stomach clenched. She'd be leaving Jasper behind when she moved on. He'd remain in Brownsville teaching more WASP how to fly. And all she'd have were good memories of being back together. Well, not exactly together, but at least friends. They'd settled into an easy camaraderie, laughing and talking about everything. Mornings began with a cup of coffee, and evenings were spent in a communal dinner.

If she didn't know better, she'd say they were dating. But he'd only formally asked her out once, other times merely appearing at her table during meals. She lost count of how often he'd walked her to the barracks. No, they weren't officially stepping out, but they were sure spending a lot of time in each other's company.

Yes, she'd miss him. More than she wanted to. Why couldn't her heart cooperate and remember they were just friends?

Chapter Eleven

Casting a glance at the gray sky, Jasper blew out a breath. Evelyn had done well yesterday during her inaugural ride in the P-51. Her landing had been bumpy, but better than most first-time pilots of the plane. More proof she was an exceptional pilot, one of the best he'd seen, and that included his male compatriots.

Very little flustered her, and she seemed to take difficulties in stride. She'd been like a child on Christmas morning when they'd approached the aircraft. If he hadn't been around, she would probably have skipped the entire distance. He smiled at the memory of the joy on her face when she'd slid into the cockpit.

Her hands settled into position on the yoke, and she'd memorized the instruments' positions within moments. Each plane had its own vagaries, but she seemed to figure out the pursuit plane's immediately.

Jasper checked his watch. She was due any minute for another flight so she could add to her hours. He picked up his pace as he headed toward the aircraft parked outside the hangar. The sun emerged from behind a cloud and glimmered on the polished silver fuselage.

Motion from inside the cockpit caught his attention and he laughed. Evelyn was already suited up and inside. Why was he surprised? She'd have slept in the plane if allowed.

He waved at her, and she grinned, her face almost as bright as the metal of the aircraft. He climbed onto the wing then leaned into the cockpit. "Someone was up early."

Her face pinked. "Is it okay that I'm here? I wanted to spend more time getting familiar with the interior. I did okay yesterday, but my reaction time was slower than I would have liked. I want to respond instinctively, and that didn't happen."

"Always the overachiever." He snorted a laugh. "Spend all the time you want as long as no one else is scheduled. But give yourself some leeway. It takes time to learn each aircraft."

"I know I'm impatient, but the sooner I learn, the sooner I can start ferrying these babies. Men need them. The war needs them."

He squeezed her shoulder. She turned toward him, and the floral scent of her shampoo wafted toward him. His heart thumped, and he licked his lips. "You can't win the war singlehandedly."

"No, but more rumors about disbanding us are trickling through the ranks. I don't know how much longer I have to fly. To help."

"Let's take it one day at a time." He raised his head and studied the sky. "I'm assuming you got the weather report. What did it say?"

"Scattered clouds. Wind five knots. Good visibility and about a twenty percent chance of rain." She shrugged. "Not great, but not too bad."

A shiver slithered up his spine. What if the forecast was wrong, and a serious storm was in the making? Evelyn was an able pilot, but even the most experienced flyer could make mistakes or crash because of conditions beyond his or her control.

The saboteur had not been found yet. Commander Lynch and the MPs had questioned Corporal Vance extensively and were convinced he was not their man. Jasper rubbed the back of his neck. Should he insist that Evelyn have the fuel in the tanks tested before she took off? Yeah, she'd have plenty to say if he suggested that.

He needed to mind his own business. As her instructor and a senior member of the flight team, he should ensure her safety, but would he go to such great lengths if another student were sitting in the P-51? In all honesty, no.

"Jasper? You're a million miles away. Is there anything you want to review before I take her up?" Evelyn's brow was creased, and her mouth set in a slash. "I'd like to get going."

"Ah, of course." He shook his head. "But I'm concerned about the weather."

She tilted her head and narrowed her eyes. "Forecast said a slight chance of rain. Since when do you care about a little moisture?"

"Well, these Texas storms can be unpredictable. Are you sure the possibility is only twenty percent?"

"That's the report I was given. If you've got a question, perhaps you should call the office. What's this all about? You're as nervous as a first-time father."

"No, I'm not. I'm simply trying to ensure your safety. You'll be hurtling through the air at incredible speed, and the elements can affect your performance. This is no Piper Cub or Vultee."

"Thank goodness for that." She wore a wry smile. "I'm ready for this flight. I've got nearly seven hundred hours racked up. More than almost everyone in the program. I'll be fine."

"Wouldn't you rather fly the smaller planes? Or become an instructor? You'd be great at teaching others how to fly. Performing missions and flying untested aircraft is dangerous."

"I'm well aware of the danger, Jasper." Her voice was cold. "I don't understand your sudden reticence about my being in the program. Your attitude hearkens back to our college days when you criticized my desire to fly. I thought you'd changed."

"I have changed." He swallowed. He'd vocalized his concerns and made her angry. She had every right to be upset, but he couldn't get past the dread at the thought of her taking the P-51 up today. Was it a premonition or simply his own fears? "I have changed," he repeated. "I'm sorry if I'm upsetting you, but I want you to fully understand what you're getting into by flying this aircraft."

"And you plan to convince me by suggesting I fly a different aircraft? An interesting use of persuasion. Maybe you'd like me to choose a plane with training wheels or I could just taxi around the tarmac for a bit, pretending to fly."

"No, I—"

Her eyes glittered, and she scowled. "Maybe I'm reading meaning into your words, but I don't think so. I'm getting the distinct impression you don't want me to certify on the P-51. Perhaps you don't think I'm capable, or maybe you do still feel that women shouldn't be pilots, but whatever your reason, you're wrong. I've been given permission to learn this plane, and I will. Are you going to teach me or not?"

Jasper blew out a deep breath. "I can teach you." He winced. His tone sounded unconvincing even to his own ears.

"That's it. We're done here. Whether I like it or not, you're the same misogynistic oaf you were ten years ago. People can't change. Why did I think you could?" She tore off her headset and unstrapped her seat belt. "You know, Jasper, one day women will be allowed to do the same jobs that men do. I may not see it in my lifetime, but it will happen. Women are competent now. We've proved we can do a great number of things no one thought we could."

She stood up and pushed him out of the way as she climbed out of the cockpit then jumped to the ground. "Do you really think God made women dumber than men? You're an engineer...a scientist. Do you have any proof that women have smaller, less capable brains?" She stomped her foot. "I don't believe we're a good training match. I'm going to request another instructor. Go find another student to antagonize." She pivoted and stalked away.

His jaw hung open, and he clamped it shut. She'd given him what for, and he'd deserved it. He'd let his emotions for her cloud his judgment. He should have remained aloof and kept his opinions to himself. He'd messed up big time. Would he have an opportunity to make amends, or would she fly out of his life in a cloud of bad feelings?

Chapter Twelve

"Come!"

Evelyn's heart thudded in her chest as she entered Commander Lynch's office. If his voice was any indication, he was not happy with the interruption or her, or perhaps both. She licked her dry lips and stood at attention in front of the man's desk.

He peered at her over his glasses, his gaze sharp and piercing.

Now she knew how a bug under a microscope felt. She straightened her spine and met his stare with one of her own. In for a penny, in for a pound.

"What can I do for you, Reid?"

"Uh, I'm here to request a different flight instructor, sir."

"Is there a problem with the one you have? Is he unavailable?"

"It's...well, we're—"

"Spit it out. I haven't got all day." He tossed his pen onto the desk and crossed his arms, a frown creasing his forehead.

"There are difficulties. I don't believe Captain MacPherson is the best instructor for me."

Commander Lynch bolted upright. "Has he been inappropriate? After how he reacted to Corporal Vance's behavior? I'll—"

"No, sir. He's not done anything wrong, exactly."

"Then what has he done. Exactly."

Her tongue stuck to the roof of her mouth, and she cleared her throat. She was doing an abysmal job of stating her case. "He's been judgmental and critical, and at times, downright rude. His training style is overbearing."

"He's hurt your feelings? Is that it? You can't handle a little abrasiveness, Reid?" The commander shook his head. "Captain MacPherson is an excellent pilot and top-notch instructor. Just because he's a little rough around the edges and offends your delicate sensibilities is not an acceptable reason to assign you a different instructor."

Evelyn sighed. She was going to be stuck with Jasper for the remainder of her stay.

"You're associated with the military, young lady, and we're not all teacups and crumpets here. We've all got to work together. Liking someone isn't part of the equation. He'll keep you alive with his knowledge. You need to get a grip on your *feelings* and listen to his instruction. Clear?"

"Yes, sir."

"I was against women pilots from the very beginning." His lips twisted in a snarl. "And this conversation proves my point. You girls allow emotions to cloud your thoughts and behaviors. A totally acceptable situation. You're dismissed, Reid, and don't let me see you in my office again for such a petty complaint."

"Thank you, sir." She pivoted on her heel and hurried from the room. What was she thinking to ask for a new instructor? She'd confirmed the CO's concerns about the WASP, and he'd lost what little respect he may have had for them—or her. She huffed out a sigh and shoved open the door, nearly barreling into Gladys.

"Oh, sorry," Evelyn squeaked. "My mistake." She ducked her head and headed toward the barracks.

"Wait." Gladys hurried to catch up with her. "What's wrong?"

Evelyn pressed her lips together and shook her head. Tears pricked the backs of her eyes. She shoved her hands into her pockets. Why did she have to cry when she was angry?"

Gladys grabbed her arm, stopping her progress. "You know I'm going to badger you until you tell me what's going on."

"Okay. But let's get inside first." They continued to the barracks then went into Evelyn's room. She dropped onto the cot, and Gladys sat beside her. Rubbing her damp hands on her pants, Evelyn shrugged. "I've ruined things for the girls." Her chin trembled. "Jasper and I were in the P-51. Well, I was in the cockpit, and he was on the wing giving me pointers. It felt like I was getting a handle on the information, and the next thing I knew, he was telling me I shouldn't fly pursuit planes...that I should consider being an instructor or fly the smaller planes."

"Really? What brought that on?"

"I don't know." Evelyn shrugged. "He seemed agitated, and the more he talked, the madder I got. Anyway, I climbed out, went to the CO, and asked him for a different instructor."

"Hmm. Bet that didn't go over well."

"Not in the least. He doesn't want us at the base and said I'd confirmed his suspicions that women can't handle difficult situations." She flopped face-first on her pillow. "I'm such an idiot."

Gladys patted her back. "Perhaps going to Commander Lynch wasn't the best idea you've had, but I doubt you've wrecked his opinion of us. Sounds like he already has a low impression of the program." She tugged on Evelyn's shoulder. "But I want to hear more about Captain MacPherson. Sounds like neither of you can put aside your past hurts, and it doesn't take much to set off either one of you."

Evelyn sat up and pulled a hanky from the nightstand. She wiped her eyes and sniffled. "He's awful, Gladys. Always making me second-guess my thoughts. One minute he seems proud of my accomplishments, and the next it seems like he wants me to do something safe and easy. I don't understand."

"Don't you?" Gladys giggled and rolled her eyes. "You two have got to be the blindest people I've ever seen. You're still in love. Both of you. He wants to keep you safe and sound, and you're not sure what to do with that information. Your pride rears up at the thought of needing a protector, yet you want to be cherished, and that's scaring you to death."

"No, absolutely not. I don't have feelings for him."

"You keep telling yourself that, honey."

Evelyn's pulse raced. "What if I do still love him? We've already tried to be a couple. It didn't work. He wants a kind of woman that I can't be."

"Maybe he's changed. Is he truly as overbearing as he was in college? Or is he trying to make an effort to understand and accept who you are?"

"I don't know." Evelyn pulled on her lower lip. "Maybe. But do you think people can change? Could he be a different person, or will we always fall back into the same arguments?"

"Answer me this. Have you changed since college?"

"I think so. At least I hope so, but what drives me is the same; my belief system is the same. That's why I can't believe that what he thinks is any different."

Gladys squeezed her hand. "But you don't *know* for certain. You need to ask yourself some hard questions. First of all, do you want a relationship with him because, to me, it seems like you might. Second, have you two discussed why you broke up? Third, ask him some hard questions about what he believes. Like I said before, I think he's trying to keep you safe, not constrained. What has he said about your skills?"

"That I'm one of the best pilots he knows." She ducked her head and plucked at her flight suit.

"Aha. That proves my point. He doesn't want to lose you. What we do is dangerous, and he knows that better than anyone." She crossed her arms and sent Evelyn a satisfied smile. "Yep, he's a love-struck schoolboy and doesn't know how to tell you."

Memories of time spent with Jasper over the last three weeks flooded Evelyn's mind. His emerald eyes sparkling when she'd grasped a concept, his warm hand squeezing her shoulder from behind when she'd executed a tricky maneuver in the aircraft, his face lined with concern when he thought she'd been injured. A touch here, a smile there.

Was it possible that he cared for her as he once did? She swallowed. If so, what in the world should she do with the information?

Chapter Thirteen

Sunlight glinted off the cockpit canopy, and Evelyn squinted at the instrument panel. As he had two days ago, Jasper stood on the wing of the P-51 looking over her shoulder. Two days during which she had time to think about her conversation with Gladys. Two days to remember the embarrassing visit to the commander's office and his disdainful stare. Her face heated, and it had nothing to do with the scorching Texas temperatures.

The crisp aroma of Jasper's aftershave wafted past her nose on the breeze. She closed her eyes and inhaled. Good thing they weren't in the air, or she'd be overcome with his scent and forget to fly. He reached toward the dashboard and pointed to the altimeter. His arm brushed her shoulder, and she trembled. Good grief. This was a training session, not a date.

"Are you okay?" A crease appeared between his eyebrows, his eyes the color of new moss.

"Yes." She slumped in the seat. "Listen, you obviously know the CO didn't grant my request for a different instructor which is why we're here, and I appreciate you not throwing his decision in my face."

"I wouldn't do that, Evie." He sent her a wry smile. "I've been thinking about what happened and realize my words made you believe I question your capabilities. I don't. You're an excellent pilot." He sighed. "But I worry about you in the air, and not because you can't handle yourself."

Evelyn's heart softened. "Thanks for saying that. It means a lot." She sighed. "I'm sorry for getting angry. I...uh...overreacted. I shouldn't have said what I did or gone to the CO. There are so many naysayers about our program...and me...I hear criticism where there isn't any."

He tapped her nose. "I thought as the redhead I'm supposed to be the one with the temper."

She chuckled. "That wouldn't be fair." Their easy banter was reminiscent of their early days in college when they hung on each other's words, thoughts, and dreams. He'd made her feel special, and she thought the sky was the limit. Until it wasn't. She shook her head. Every time she remembered the past, negative thoughts crowded forward to block out the good memories. Why? Anger? Fear? Another reason? Their time together here was a new chapter. Why couldn't she leave the previous chapter behind?

"I think you're all set, Evie. Why don't you take her out for an hour?"

"Thanks, Jasper. It's a perfect day for hanging about in the clouds. I'm sorry you can't go with me."

"Oh, did I leave that part out?" He winked and pointed to a nearby P-51. "I'm joining you up there. Granted, I won't get to be your copilot, but formation flying is the next best thing. Not sure that you need it, but you can get more practice hours on the books."

"Perfect." Evelyn grinned. "Try to keep up."

"No problem." Jasper cupped her cheek for a quick moment then ran his finger along her jaw. "See you up there." He hopped off the wing and strode toward the other aircraft.

Her skin tingled where he'd touched her, and she put her hand to her face. Her breath hitched.

"P-51 Reid, you are cleared for takeoff. Please use runway two." Static crackled as the controller's voice blared through her headset.

She blinked at the interruption and exhaled. "Roger that, control tower." She headed for the runway, passing Jasper's aircraft. He waved and gave her a thumbs-up, a sloppy grin on his face. How wonderful to know someone who loved flying as much as she did. Someone who understood the thrill of lifting off and riding among the clouds. She returned his gesture and taxied the remaining distance to the runway.

Aware of Jasper bringing up the rear, she went through the motions to take the plane airborne. Minutes later, she was aloft and winging away from the base. The engine droned a steady rumble as she penciled the takeoff time on the patch of adhesive tape stuck to the knee of her coveralls for that purpose. Motion to her right grabbed her attention, and Jasper was beside her still wearing the silly smile.

They circled the base, and she concentrated on maintaining a correct distance from his aircraft. She wended her way through cotton-ball clouds. Still vigilant, she managed to relax as she got the hang of holding steady mere meters from the other plane. The majestic beauty of the sky never ceased to cause her heart to pound and create a desire to bow her head in worship.

"Lord, thank You for this chance to fly and experience Your creation from above. Words can't express what's in my heart." Warmth settled on her shoulders, and she smiled. "It's just You and me in here, so I guess now is as good a time as any to talk to You about Jasper...and everything that's been going on. Gladys has stirred up a lot of thoughts about him and the past and a possible future. But I'm scared. No, correct that. I'm terrified. Flying is who I am, and I sure would hate to have that taken away."

She glanced out the cockpit at Jasper's plane. Still holding constant. Like he promised. Had he always been there? Was she the one to pull away?

"What are You saying, Father? Are You putting these conclusions in my head? Did You arrange my path so that Jasper and I would be here together? So many questions. I don't want to run ahead of You anymore. I've been doing that a lot. I'm happier when I'm following You, but then I push myself out front." She snorted a laugh. "Maybe I should do all my praying in a plane. Life is so much clearer up here, Lord, but I guess I can't stay in the sky forever. What do you want of me?"

Follow, My child.

"To where?"

Follow Me.

Evelyn giggled. "You're going to keep me guessing, aren't You, Lord? Okay, I'll follow You." Tension slipped from her shoulders, and tears welled. Why couldn't she remember the peace she received from resting in God? Instead, she raced ahead then wondered at the confusion and hurt that seemed to nip her heels.

She glanced at the clock on the instrument panel, and her eyes widened. Her hour was nearly complete, yet had passed in a flash. "Reid to MacPherson, are you ready to return to base?"

"Roger that. See you on the ground." His voice seemed to caress her through the headset.

Oh boy. She had to get a grip and not just on the control wheel. She pressed her lips together and prepared the aircraft for landing as she focused her eyes on the distant runway. She dropped her altitude and approached the black strip of macadam. Lower. Lower. The craft hovered above the ground as she slowed her speed. Wheels squealing, she landed and pressed the brakes. Scenery rushed past in a blur of green and brown. As the plane slowed, she rotated her neck to survey the base. "Thank You for another safe landing, Lord." The aircraft came to a stop, and she taxied toward the hangar.

One of the ground crew waved her to a location, and she parked the plane. Several minutes later, Jasper's plane was beside hers, and he was climbing to the ground. He trotted toward her. "Great job on formation. I'm impressed."

Her heart swelled. "Thanks." Why did his opinion mean so much? Ugh. She was overthinking things again. "Want to grab a cup of joe or some ice tea? I'm parched."

"Sounds great."

"Captain MacPherson?"

She and Jasper turned toward a corporal who stood at attention near the hangar door. Jasper tilted his head. "Yes?"

The young man handed him a sheet of paper then saluted and headed inside.

Jasper glanced at the page then handed it to her. "This concerns you, too. We've been ordered to compile a report on the WASP statistics. How their performance compares to the guys...that sort of thing."

She stiffened. Was the military looking for proof to disband the program, like the rumors said? Were her days as a ferry pilot coming to an end?

Follow.

Oops. All that time in the air promising God she'd follow him, and at the first sign of a problem, she was off and running. She forced a smile. "Okay, but first my coffee."

He smiled, his eyes sparkling in the sunlight. "Absolutely. We need something to keep us awake during the project. By the way, you should know that statistics was my worst subject in school. I hope you can pick up the slack."

More time with Jasper. Her pulse skipped. She'd miss him when she left, but for now she'd revel in every moment she was able to spend with him. She'd deal with the ramifications to her heart later.

Chapter Fourteen

Jasper rubbed the back of his neck then stretched his arms over his head. His spine crackled, and Evelyn glanced at him, her eyes wide. He shrugged. "Guess these old bones are protesting the amount of time I'm spending hunched over files." He shoved aside the pile he'd been studying. "I don't know about you, but I could use a break."

She nodded. "How about a walk around the base?"

"No." He shook his head. "I've got something better in mind. I'll put this stuff away, and you go change into something you don't mind getting dirty."

Her eyebrow lifted. "Are we going to the maintenance shed?"

"Ha. I want to show you some of the sights, and they might involve sand between your toes."

Evelyn clapped her hands. "The beach? Oh, Jasper. I can't remember the last time I went to the ocean." She jumped up. Her chair fell backward and hit the floor. Cheeks red, she bent to set it upright. "Are you sure you don't want any help?" Her voice was breathless.

He smiled. What would it be like to make her this happy all the time? "Go." He checked his watch. "Meet me at the front gate in thirty minutes."

She waved and rushed from the room, her ebony ponytail dancing.

Yes, he could get used to making her face light up. He rose and stacked the paperwork on the corner of his desk then picked up the telephone to make arrangements with the motor pool. Vehicle secured, he hurried to the mess hall to grab a couple of colas and some snacks. The clock overhead told him there was enough time to head to his quarters to put on a fresh shirt. Whistling, he hurried to the barracks, changed his clothes, then headed to pick up the Indian Scout he'd checked out. Stuffing the food into one of the leather saddlebags, he jumped on the motorcycle and gunned the engine.

"Someone's got a date." The sergeant in charge of the vehicles clutched his clipboard and grinned at Jasper, shouting over the roar, "No one is that happy to take out one of the bikes."

"It's not a date. Just two friends out for a pleasure ride."

"Uh-huh. Whatever you say. Just have it back on time."

"Will do. Thanks again, Sarge."

"You'll just owe me a favor, and I'll let you know when I need something." A wolfish gleam shimmered in the sergeant's eyes.

Jasper nodded and drove toward the gate. Evelyn stood next to the guard shack looking cute and fresh as a daisy in lightweight tan slacks and a white sleeveless blouse. Her raven-black hair glistened in the sun. Right.

Just two friends. He exhaled and pulled up beside her. "Hop on and hold tight."

Hesitating, she eyed the motorcycle for a moment then shrugged and climbed onto the bike. She wrapped her arms around his middle, and his heart beat an uneven tattoo in his chest. He let out the clutch and accelerated off the base. Too late now, but a jeep might have been a better choice of vehicle. She would have been safely seated beside him instead of snuggled against his back.

The wind in his face was hot and dry as he sped along the road leading toward the water. The bike ate up the miles, and before long they made it to Port Isabel. He slowed the vehicle and turned north on a side street. Moments later, they stopped. He parked the cycle and dug into the saddlebag for their food before leading her to the grassy parklike area on the shores of the peninsula.

They sat on the ground, and he popped open the colas then handed her one. He gestured to the barrier island in the distance. "I'd like to have shown you Padre Island, but the military has made it off limits to civilians. Even though I'm in the air force, I didn't want to push my luck by asking permission to hold a picnic." He took a swig of soda. "Besides that, they've got a bunch of target practice sites. Having to run for cover might put a damper on the day."

She snickered then took a deep breath as she slipped off her shoes. "This is perfect. I can already feel the tension slipping away. I prefer the sky, but this view is the next best thing. How do you know what they're doing on the island?"

"The CO told me during an early meeting for flight-planning purposes. The crazy thing is that there are still thousands of cattle over there." He removed his shoes and socks then rolled up his pant legs. "Practice is suspended during the annual roundup, but the rest of the time, the animals wander at will. One of the guys told me they graze the ranges when it's quiet but move out of the area when they hear the planes."

"Guess cows are smarter than I give them credit for." She sipped her drink. "What else can you tell me, Mr. Tour Guide?"

He slid his gaze to her. Was she mocking him? Her eyes sparkled with curiosity, and he leaned back on his elbows. "I'm glad you asked because the island's history is interesting, having been owned by four countries since being discovered. Spain had it first, then Mexico got the land after the Revolution. When Texas became a republic they claimed a bunch of land that included the island. Then we acquired it after our war with Mexico in the mid-eighteen hundreds."

"You're a wealth of knowledge, Professor." She grinned. "Is that the end of today's lesson?"

Snorting a laugh, he poked her ribs. "There's plenty more where that came from, and there will be a quiz later."

Her laughter rang out like wind chimes, and he poked her again. She squirmed away from his reach, but he stretched his arm and tickled her. She shrieked, jumped up and ran toward the laguna separating the island from the mainland. He leapt to his feet and chased her, giving her enough space to think he couldn't catch her. She danced at the edge of the water, a wide smile lighting up her face.

He made a show of wiping his forehead and pretended to breathe heavily as if tired. Her stance relaxed, and he charged at her. Grabbing her around the waist, he picked her up and walked into the lapping waves. Her squeal pierced his ears, and he winced, but continued to hold her. The crisp aroma of soap wafted from her skin, and he breathed in her scent.

"Don't you dare drop me, Jasper." Her voice had a glint of steel.

"I wouldn't dream of it, but I am enjoying the moment." He winked then grinned when she reddened to the roots of her hair.

"You're incorrigible." She continued to wiggle in his arms then went limp, her eyes fluttering closed.

A chill swept over him. "Are you okay?" He hurried from the water and laid her on the sand. His heart skittered.

Her eyes flew open, and she sat up. "Gotcha!"

"You little imp." He picked her up and slung her over his shoulder. "Now, you're really going to get it." He ran back to the water's edge as she pounded on his back and tried to free herself from his grasp. He guffawed. "Is that the best you've got?"

"You're going to be sorry."

"I have no doubt." He whirled around then walked back to their spot on the grass and set her down. He took one of her hands and brought it to his lips. "Please forgive me, m'lady. I was caught up in the moment."

Evelyn dipped her head then sent him a mocking glare, but a smile tugged at the corners of her mouth, belying her anger.

Still holding her hand, he tucked it in the crook of his elbow then gently tugged her forward. They strolled along the shore. Seagulls swooped on the thermals overhead, their strident cries mingling with the sound of the waves. Sometimes talking, other times allowing silence to envelop them, Jasper and Evelyn wandered along the bank. An hour passed. Then two.

Finally, he couldn't avoid the knowledge that it was time to turn around, climb on the bike, and head back to reality. His stomach clenched. There was work to be done, and their respite was over. The war had brought them back together but not for long. She'd move on to her next assignment. But the afternoon had been a sweet escape, one he'd remember long after she was gone. If only they didn't have to part.

Chapter Fifteen

Arms wrapped around Jasper's waist, Evelyn perched on the back of the motorcycle. The buzz of the engine roared in her ears, and the uneven road jolted her spine as the miles passed. "Are you going to hit every bump?" she shouted to be heard above the motor.

Jasper grinned and steered the bike back and forth in a wide S pattern.

She screeched and tightened her grip. His body vibrated with laughter against her. Swatting his shoulder, she closed her eyes. They'd be fine. He was an excellent pilot. Surely that translated into being an able driver.

He pointed to a distant field crowded with cattle, their umber-colored forms blurry against the yellow-green pasture. Puffy white clouds scudded across the sky overhead. A red-tailed hawk circled then swooped down and grabbed a tiny rodent in its talons. Jasper's tangy aftershave mingled with the warm Texas breeze.

The afternoon had been filled with blissful silence walking ankle deep in the surf followed by extensive conversations about their lives in the decade since college. They'd both been candid about their missteps and failures. Evelyn's face heated. Jasper had been gracious about the more embarrassing incidents, but regret clung to her nonetheless.

What would it be like to pursue a relationship with him? To heed Gladys's advice and see where the future would take them as a couple? Her stomach hollowed. What if that's not what he had in mind? He'd been fun and flirty today, but that didn't mean he was interested in dating. Maybe he was trying to make up for their bickering. Maybe he was lonely, and since they had history, he decided spending time with her was easier than getting to know someone new.

Could they pick up where they left off? Could they shed their hurt and anger? Today made it seem possible. She pressed her lips together. Speculation was useless. The rules against a WASP dating an instructor were clear and unbreakable, and after she was finished training, she'd be sent elsewhere. Tough to date when the man and woman weren't in the same location. She'd wanted California. Now, the sunny coastal state seemed too far away.

They approached the outskirts of the town, and she frowned. How had the trip back been quicker than the journey to the water?

The bike coughed and hesitated. Jasper revved the throttle, but the engine hiccuped then quit. The cycle slowed, and he wheeled it to the shoulder of the road before braking. They climbed off, and Evelyn blew out a breath. Hopefully, he could fix the problem. Her knowledge of motorcycle mechanics fit on the head of a pin, although maybe they weren't that different from airplane mechanics.

Jasper pulled a small leather pouch from the saddlebag then squatted next to the bike. He poked and prodded connections and various parts, mumbling as he worked.

She shielded her eyes and searched the highway for oncoming traffic. Nothing. She wandered toward him. "Anything I can do to help?"

"Nope. I should have it fixed in a jiffy."

"You should have performed a preflight check on the bike before signing it out." She nudged his shoulder. "Every good pilot does that."

"You could have done a better job of selecting our ride?" He chuckled. "And just how much do you know about bikes?"

Evelyn grinned and tilted her head. "Admittedly, not much."

"I'm going to claim this is the government's fault. They probably went with the low bidder."

"Maybe, but I've heard that the Indian brand rivals Harley, so maybe the mechanic missed something." She froze. "Or maybe this is more sabotage."

His eyes widened, then he shook his head. "I've known the sergeant for a long time. He went through basic with me then was at the air base in England for a while when I was stationed there. He's always been a stand-up guy. Even if this is his doing, would he be dumb enough to be the one to check out the vehicle to me?"

"True. I guess I'm jumping at shadows. It's hard to know who to trust."

"I understand, and I'm not totally discounting the possibility." He went back to examining the bike then blew out a loud breath and pointed to a large crack on one of the engine parts. "I found the problem, and unless you're carrying spare parts, there's nothing we can do to make the repair."

She giggled and patted her pockets as if searching for the part. "I must have left them in my other purse."

He chuckled as he climbed to his feet. He collected the tools, slid them into the pouch, then tucked it in the saddlebag. His gaze swept the highway as hers had done moments ago. His glance flicked to her face. "Do we wait to see if someone comes by, or do we walk the bike back to base?"

"Is it too much to hope we'll be rescued?"

"Not really. Especially now that we're close to town. But maybe everyone is preparing dinner."

She fanned herself. "I'm game if you are to roll the bike. Aren't there rules about abandoning government property?"

"Probably. How about if you hop on and steer, and I'll push."

"No. Too awkward, and my added weight will make it harder."

Jasper rubbed his jaw. "Okay, then you take the right handlebar, and I'll take the left. I think we're only three or four miles from base."

"Or we could go into town and telephone for help."

"Maybe. I'll get ribbed enough for breaking down, but to ask for a pickup when all we have to do is walk will give the boys fodder for months to come."

"Good grief. The male ego truly is a fragile thing. Suit yourself." She wiped her hands on her slacks, then stepped toward the bike, and reached for the handlebar. Her foot went into a hole, and she stumbled. She lurched forward, and her arms flew out from her sides to maintain her balance. The loose soil shifted under her shoes, and she fell against Jasper with a yelp.

His hands grabbed her shoulders to keep her upright then slipped around her back.

Face burning, she looked up with a nervous laugh. "Thanks. I...uh...not my most graceful moment."

His pupils dilated, creating thin emerald rings around the black circles.

Her breath hitched at his piercing expression, and she swallowed, mouth suddenly dry as a Texas desert.

His gaze flicked to her lips then back to her eyes. One hand drew lazy circles on her back, and with the other he tugged off the band that held her ponytail. Free from its confines, her dark locks encircled her face. He tucked the band into his pocket then ran his fingers through her hair, still searching her face.

Evelyn trembled. Was he going to kiss her? Did she want him to? This would not be a nervous first kiss. She already knew the feel of his mouth on hers and how perfectly they fit on hers. Her pulse thumped erratically. Could he feel her heart jumping?

He lowered his head a fraction, hesitating, his eyes probing hers, asking the question: would she accept his kiss?

She rose on her toes and closed the distance, pressing her lips to his. She closed her eyes, giving herself fully to the kiss. She may not have a future with Jasper, but she would tell him without words how much he meant to her. That he still held a special place in her heart, and she was incomplete without him. That she loved him.

Love? Is that what she was feeling? It couldn't be. One day of playful banter didn't translate into love. Did it?

He tightened his embrace.

Tingles swept over her, and she wrapped her arms around him, her hands clinging to his back. She'd been cradled in his grasp before. In the past. But today's embrace felt different. Rather than two young college students, they were mature adults who'd experienced highs and lows...good and bad. Who knew that life could be snuffed out in a moment, yet choosing not to be cavalier with the time they'd been granted.

Sweetness. That's what was different. Jasper's kiss tasted sweet and made her feel...what was the word Gladys had used...cherished. Yes.

He pulled back and pressed his forehead to hers.

She sighed. If this wasn't love...who was she kidding...the feeling washing over her was love. Pure and simple. Too bad a relationship would never work.

Chapter Sixteen

The distant hum of a car engine floated on the hot, dry air, and Jasper looked over Evelyn's shoulder at the approaching truck. "Someone's coming. Perhaps they can help us."

She pulled away and turned, smoothing her hair then straightening her shoulders.

He waved his arms over his head and squinted against the glare of the late afternoon sun on the vehicle's windshield. Would the driver stop?

The rumble grew louder.

Evelyn stood next to the bike, arms crossed, a look of uncertainty on her face.

Did she regret their kiss? Unfortunately, the truck's untimely appearance didn't allow time to talk about it. At least they might not have to push the motorcycle for miles.

An ancient black Ford pickup freckled with rust spots pulled off the road and braked. Jasper jogged to the passenger side and stuck his head through the window. The driver, a wizened, gray-haired man gestured to the bike. "Havin' trouble?"

"Yes, a part in the engine has cracked, and we're on our way back to the airfield. Would you be able to take us and the cycle to the base? We could pay you for the gas."

"Be happy to, and you're one of our boys in the service, so no need to give me money. Let me give you a hand with puttin' the bike in the back."

"That's okay. I've got it."

"I may be older than the hills, but there's life in me yet, young man." He climbed out of the truck and walked toward the motorcycle, his steps sure and spry. He touched the brim of his baseball cap. "Howdy, miss."

Jasper's face heated. Nothing like insulting his only chance for a lift. He hurried to the bike and grabbed one of the handlebars. "I'm Captain Jasper MacPherson. This is Miss Evelyn Reid. Thank you for your assistance."

The old man nodded. "Name's Dexter Quimby. You can call me Dex. No need to stand on ceremony."

"Well, Dex, we appreciate your help."

"Glad to. You one of them pilots I see zooming around up there?" He gestured to the sky. "Those planes are something else."

"Sometimes. I mostly teach other pilots how to fly. Miss Reid is one of our ferry pilots."

Dex blinked. "Girl pilots. We'll I'll be. Good for you, missy. We fought on the ground and in the water during the Spanish-American war.

That was a nasty bit of business. But worse was the war with the Philippines that started the next year." He frowned. "Lost more than a few buddies in that one."

"I'm sorry about your friends."

"Thanks. I'll bet you've lost a few of your own."

Jasper nodded and swallowed the lump in his throat.

They wheeled the bike to the back of the truck and laid it down in the bed. Dex brushed his hands together then jerked his head toward the front of the vehicle. "Might be kind of cozy, but there's room for both of you."

"Thank you, Mr. Quim—Dex." Evelyn smiled and climbed into the truck.

Dex grinned and nodded as he slid into the driver's seat. "Anytime, missy."

Jasper sat next to Evelyn. Cozy was a generous term for the amount of space they had. He was jammed against the door, yet his leg and side grazed hers every time he moved. Dex's arms were tucked close to his sides as he gripped the steering wheel.

The truck pulled onto the highway and gained speed. Dex glanced at Evelyn. "Which of them planes do you fly? The big ones or the little ones?"

"Both, but I'm here to learn how to fly the pursuit planes—the ones that escort the bombers. We women ferry the aircraft from the factories and bases to wherever they need to go for the men to use them."

"Been flying long?"

"Yes, sir. I got my license when I was in high school, and I've been flying ever since. I owned a crop dusting company before joining the WASP."

He winked. "You don't look much older than my nineteen-year-old granddaughter."

Evelyn flushed. "That's kind of you to say, but I'm significantly older than her."

Jasper grinned. The old geezer was apparently a ladies' man. Evelyn shifted, and her leg rubbed his. Her quick intake of breath told him all he needed to know. She was as aware of his body as he was of hers. The two miles back to base would be excruciating, and he'd enjoy every second of it.

Several minutes later, the truck stopped in front of the gate. Dex hopped out and waved to the guards then circled to the back of the truck as Jasper and Evelyn stepped from the vehicle. Jasper helped Dex retrieve the bike from the bed before grabbing the handlebars. "Thank you, sir. If there's anything you ever need, don't hesitate to contact the base."

The old man nodded then bowed to Evelyn. "A pleasure to meet you, young lady. You keep flying them planes and showing the boys what for." With a jaunty gait, he headed to the truck and climbed inside.

"What gives, Captain?" One of the guards stood at attention, an M1 Garand propped on his shoulder.

"We've got a crack in the engine."

"Bet you're glad the old guy came along."

"Yep. Would have been a long trek."

Evelyn grabbed one of the handlebars and helped him wheel the bike toward the motor pool. The sergeant would not be happy to see the damaged vehicle.

She blew out a deep breath and grinned. "You sure know how to show a girl a good time."

"I'm glad you enjoyed yourself." He chuckled. "Lots of planning went into the afternoon."

"Seems like it."

"Listen, Evie, before we get to the garage, shouldn't we talk about what happened back there? We need to figure out where we are in this relationship."

"What is there to talk about? We kissed. End of story."

His spine stiffened. "What do you mean end of story? That kiss was more than a peck on the cheek. You responded to me. Do you deny that it meant something?"

"Yes, I responded. Your kisses move me. They always have, but that doesn't mean there's a relationship. There can't be."

"But why not?" He cringed at the whining tone in his voice.

"Number one: I'm leaving as soon as training is over. I'll be stationed somewhere far away—"

"Plenty of folks have long-distance relation—"

"I know, but we couldn't make one work when we were together. How will we be successful if we're apart? Besides, we still have the same problem we did years ago. Our philosophies don't line up. You made your position clear when you intimated I should be an instructor or something less dangerous. Face it, you don't agree with me being a pilot."

"I've changed. Yes. I was an oaf during college, but I'm no longer that man. It's not that I don't want you to fly planes. It's just that...well...I'm terrified of something happening to you, so I say things I shouldn't." He twisted his lips into a wry smile. "And then you get mad, and I'm left fumbling with an apology."

"I'm sorry, Jasper, but I don't want to talk about this anymore. Even if you have changed..." She pressed her lips together and shook her head.

"Okay, so you don't want to talk about it, then just listen. I think we have the potential for something special, and I believe we can make it work. I will prove to you that we belong together. Do you even wonder why neither of us have married? I don't wonder because I know we're supposed to be together. I am a better man when I'm with you, Evie, and I hope I make you a better person. I don't know if God handpicks mates for people, but I feel like He gave us to each other." He tugged the bike away from her. "I'll take care of the motorcycle. Please take some time and think about what I've said."

"I can't make any promises that I'll agree with you." Tears shimmered in her eyes.

"Just give me a fair shake. That's all I'm asking." He wheeled the bike toward the garage. It took all his strength not to turn back and look at her.

Chapter Seventeen

The P-51 hit the ground and bounced. And bounced again. Evelyn cringed as she braked the aircraft. Her worst landing ever. Even when she was a student pilot, she hadn't brought down a plane so hard. Jasper would be waiting for her near the hangar. What would he say about her shoddy performance? Had their conversation from yesterday haunted his thoughts as it had plagued hers? He didn't mention it before her flight, although he appeared distracted.

She brought the plane to a stop and then taxied to the steel garage. Wearing his dress uniform, he stood at the doorway. His slouch hat covered hair that would have glistened in the sun if uncovered. The brim of his cover shielded his emerald eyes, but a smile clung to his lips. Perhaps he'd missed seeing her come down.

With quick motions, she turned off the engine, popped the cockpit canopy, and unstrapped herself. She climbed over the rim and onto the wing then jumped to the ground, her parachute banging against her legs.

He lifted one hand in greeting and remained inside. She hurried to him, her heart pounding. She was usually exhilarated after a flight. Today she was exhausted. She extricated herself from the parachute and dropped it on the ground. "That wasn't my prettiest landing."

"There was a slight crosswind. I figured the breeze caught you." He shrugged. "Besides they can't all be perfect."

"Why not?" She cocked her head and grinned. "What's up with the outfit? Going somewhere?"

"Yes, and so are you."

"Yeah, to lie down. I could use some shut-eye."

Jasper picked up her parachute and gestured to a nearby jeep she hadn't noticed. "We've been invited to Deirdre and Quinn's engagement party at the officers' club. We'll zip over to the barracks so you can get cleaned up, and then we'll head over to the festivities."

She hopped into the vehicle. "He asked her to marry him? Last I heard, he'd been assigned to England, and they'd agreed to keep things light."

He put her chute in the back then slid behind the wheel and winked. "Keep up with the times, Evie. Apparently, he decided he couldn't live without her and proposed last night."

"Hmm. She seemed adamant not to get serious. Wonder what made her change her mind?"

"She loved him?"

Evelyn rolled her eyes and propped her feet on the dash. "Get me to the barracks, MacPherson."

"As you wish, ma'am." He started the jeep then sped along the macadam toward the cluster of low-slung buildings that housed the pilots.

She pulled at her fingers then crossed her arms. Why was she so agitated about Deirdre's decision?

Jasper stopped in front of Evelyn's quarters and glanced at his watch. "Thirty minutes enough time, or would you like an hour?"

"Half an hour is fine." She stepped out and grabbed her chute. "Any longer, and I might lie down and fall asleep."

"We can't have that." He chuckled and waved then pulled away.

She watched him leave, the jacket of his uniform stretching across his broad shoulders as he maneuvered the vehicle. She huffed out a loud breath and trudged into the barracks. At least Deirdre made a decision.

Evelyn headed down the corridor, unlocked her door, and entered her tiny cubicle. She tossed her parachute into the bottom of her wardrobe. Her stomach hollowed as she doffed her flight suit then slipped her arms through her dressing gown. She grabbed her soap and towel and hurried to the showers. With any luck, the pounding water would clear away the confusion in her mind and heart. She was making herself crazy with all the waffling. One minute flying was all she wanted, then she'd catch sight of Jasper, and all sense of reason fled.

The cold trickle from the showerhead chilled her, and she soaped and rinsed off with alacrity. Because of the Texas heat, she didn't need a hot shower, but the icy waters in the bathroom ensured no one took much time under the spigot.

Toweling herself dry, she poked her toes into her scuffs, then headed back to her room. She dressed quickly. Peering into the small mirror on the wall, she brushed her hair and put on her makeup. Shadows hung below her eyes, and she added powder in an effort to hide the dark smudges. Leaning close to her reflection, she frowned. Fatigue and worry clung to her features. Hopefully, the lights would be turned down in the officers' club, and no one would notice her less-than-pristine appearance. "Lighten up, Evelyn. You're going to a party."

A horn tooted outside, and she looked out the window. Tardiness had never been an issue for Jasper.

She stuffed her keys into her pocketbook, shut off the light as she left, then closed the door. The heels of her pumps clattered on the floorboards, and she slowed, but her pulse continued to skip. She straightened her spine and walked outside.

"Hey, beautiful." Jasper wiggled his eyebrows. "You clean up all right."

"You're not so bad yourself." The tension drained from her shoulders. He was his playful self. They'd have a great time together, and she'd think of nothing but dancing and chatting with her friends, not the fact that her orders would be coming soon. With only a few more hours to rack up before taking her check flight, she'd probably be at a new base within a month, maybe less.

Her steps faltered, and her neck muscles knotted. In the blink of an eye, she'd managed to drag herself back into the quagmire of indecision.

Climbing out of the jeep, Jasper offered Evelyn his elbow. "You look lovely. I'm glad you agreed to attend the party. Quinn ships out tomorrow night."

"So soon? I thought he wasn't leaving until next week." She grabbed his arm.

The warmth of her hand permeated his sleeve. Focus, man. He shook his head and helped her sit down. Her skirt scooted up, and he caught a glimpse of her shapely legs. He looked away, but the image lingered in his head. Giving himself a mental slap, he crawled behind the wheel. "As is their habit, the air force changed its mind and amended his orders."

"Poor Deidre." She smoothed her skirt. "Let's give him a send-off he won't forget."

Jasper put the jeep in gear and drove toward the officers' club. Despite the setting sun, the temperatures still hovered in the eighties, and the wind did nothing to lower the heat. How did Evelyn manage to look crisp and cool in such weather?

Minutes later, they arrived, and he parked the vehicle. Muffled music filtered out the open windows from behind the blackout curtains, mingling with laughter and the murmur of conversations. Couples and groups of men and women wandered in and out of the building.

"Hey, Evelyn!" Gladys jumped from the converted cattle truck, a broad smile on her face. She rushed toward them and winked at Jasper. "Glad you could talk her into coming. Bet she was going to stay in tonight."

"I'm right here." She waved her hand in front of Gladys's face. "You don't have to talk about me as if I'm missing in action."

"Sorry."

Jasper chuckled. Evelyn's friend looked anything but apologetic.

She linked arms with Evelyn and him. "Can't wait to kick up my heels. All I've done is study and fly. Not that I don't love flying back and forth across the good ol' U.S. of A., but a girl's got to have fun now and again."

He stole a peek at Evelyn, and his chest lightened. She seemed less agitated and apprehensive than when he'd picked her up. A perfectionist, perhaps she was still upset over her poor landing. She'd probably want to get back in the air first thing in the morning to prove to herself she was a excellent pilot. How many times had he done the same thing?

Heat from the writhing mass of dancers created an oven-like atmosphere in the room. He scanned the room and spied a vacant table in the far corner. He tugged on Gladys's arm. "Come on. I found a place to sit."

"Who wants to sit?" She resisted his move.

"We need somewhere to park our things and set our drinks."

She shrugged. "Okay."

He shouldered his way through the mob, the girls tagging along behind him like a pair of ducklings. They arrived at the table, and he shed his jacket. Gladys and Evelyn laid down their purses, and Evelyn sank into one of the chairs. He sat beside her and looked at Gladys. "Staying or going?"

With a pixie grin, she jerked her thumb toward the floor. "What do you think?" Not waiting for an answer, she whirled and melted into the crowd.

Evelyn shook her head and smiled. "Where does she get her energy? I plan to have fun, but I'm tuckered after a full day of classes and flying."

"Bet you're thirsty, too. I'll grab us something to drink." Jasper rose and threaded his way to the bar where he grabbed a couple of lemonades then returned to the table. He dropped into his seat and handed Evelyn a glass. He clinked his glass with hers. "To good friends." He chugged half the golden liquid as she took a sip. "Not to your liking?"

"It's delicious, but my mother would be horrified if I guzzled my drink."

His face warmed. "Mine, too. Pardon my lack of manners."

She giggled and waved her hand in a dismissive gesture. "Of course, our mothers haven't lived where it's one hundred and twenty degrees in the shade."

"True. Are you okay sitting here, or would you prefer to take a turn around the dance floor?"

"A dance would be lovely." She gave him a wry smile then drained her glass. "Delicious. Don't tell my mom."

He pinched his thumb and forefinger together then ran them across his mouth. "My lips are sealed." He rose and held out his hand. "Shall we?"

Flipping her hair over her shoulder, she rose and grasped his fingers.

As expected, tingles shot through his palm and up his arm. Did she feel the electricity, too? He placed his hand on her hip and pulled her toward him. Her eyes widened, and her breath caught. Maybe he had a chance after all. His pulse quickened.

The song ended, and he snorted a laugh. "So much for my timing."

Her eyes sparkled. "Give it a minute. I'm sure someone will put another coin in the jukebox."

He stared at her face that pinked under his scrutiny. Her porcelain skin held a slight sheen from the heat, and a smile tugged at the corner of her heart-shaped mouth. Her ebony hair curled around her oval face, shiny and silky looking in the bright lights. He moved his hand up her back and fingered one of the glimmering tresses. Yep, as soft as he remembered.

Her eyes widened, then Bing Crosby's "Be Careful, It's My Heart" filled the room, and relief flitted across her face.

Stupid move. He knew better than to make romantic overtures. He released her hair and began to dance. The goal for tonight was to simply show her a good time, so she'd have a memory to hang on to after she arrived at her new assignment. With any luck, she would miss him as much as he would miss her.

Would she give him the address of her posting or would she sever ties? Letters wouldn't be as effective as time together, but he could say things he'd stumble over in person. He got tongue-tied and lost all sense of reason when he looked into her eyes. Only a few more days to woo her, to convince her she couldn't live without him. He couldn't push, or she'd flee like a skittish colt.

Surely, the war wouldn't last more than another year or eighteen months. He would stay in touch, keeping his tone light and friendly. Then after the conflict was over, he could pursue her in earnest.

Would he regret waiting?

Chapter Eighteen

Evelyn drained the last of her coffee and grimaced. Lukewarm and bitter, the drink's redeeming factor was the caffeine that would keep her awake during today's class. Two days had passed since the engagement party, and she couldn't shed the feel of dancing in Jasper's arms for most of the night. They'd talked and laughed, and the hours had seemed like minutes. They'd rarely seen Gladys who had danced with every soldier and airman in the room at least twice, then allowed one lucky man to escort her to the barracks.

Despite her exhaustion and aching feet that night, Evelyn has tossed and turned until blushing peach-colored rays announced the dawn. Jasper had been gracious and attentive, never once discussing serious topics. Instead, he'd whirled and twirled her with occasional chatting about innocuous subjects like his favorite foods and what he missed about home. He'd plied her with questions about her home, too, as if he were getting to know her for the first time.

A high-pitched shriek punctuated the clatter of metal. Evelyn's head shot up. One of the new female pilots had managed to fall into the rack that held the trays and silverware, knocking everything to the floor. The poor woman's face was scarlet as a split second of silence hovered over the dining hall. Then someone clapped, and applause filled the room. Evelyn shook her head. The girl didn't deserve to be embarrassed like that, but her response would indicate the probability of her success in the WASP program.

Consternation and frustration flitted across the woman's face, then a familiar ginger-haired man rose and helped her pick up the mess. The girl smiled, her cheeks still flaming. Leave it to Jasper to aid a damsel in distress. A pair of nearby mechanics rushed to assist, probably shamed by his gallantry. One of the dishwashers brought clean dinnerware and confiscated the items that had been on the floor. In the span of five minutes, the area was cleared as if the incident hadn't occurred.

With a paper napkin, Evelyn wiped her mouth. You had to appreciate military efficiency. The young woman picked up a clean tray and scooted down the line, her head hung low. Odds were that she wouldn't last the month, perhaps even less. A shame, although if the continued rumors were to be believed, the WASP wouldn't be around much longer.

She frowned then shook her head. Latching on to speculation didn't do her any good. Better to focus on situations she could do something about...which led her back to the situation with Jasper...what to do about the feelings coursing through her veins. How could she reconcile her love of flying with a man who seemed intent on keeping her out of harm's way?

"Got a second, Evie?" Jasper stood in front of her, hat gripped between his long, tapered fingers.

"Uh...sure." She gestured to the vacant seat across from her. Good thing he wasn't a mind reader. "What's up?"

He dropped into the chair, laid down his cover, and propped his elbows on the table. He glanced around then leaned toward her. "I've received a lead on which of the mechanics may be our culprit." His voice was barely discernable above the noise in the room. "I haven't said anything to the CO because I'd rather have proof before I go to him."

"That's wonderful news. How did you get the information?"

"Believe it or not, your *friend*, Corporal Vance, came to me with the tip. He's not totally convinced, but the guy has made enough comments and innuendos. Vance said he's concerned."

"Concerned?" Evelyn lifted eyebrow. "I find that description hard to believe."

Jasper snickered. "I wasn't clear. He's concerned for his own skin. The corporal knows he's under scrutiny and doesn't want to be charged with the crimes, so he'd been very cooperative with our investigation."

She shuddered at the memory of the man's arms around her and his hot breath on her face. "So he's suddenly an upstanding citizen? I'm glad you're the one to deal with him and not me." Jasper's warm fingers squeezed her arm, and her pulse skittered. "What's your plan?"

"I'll need your help. Are you in?"

"Absolutely. I want to see this nonsense stopped. We haven't had an incident in a while, but that doesn't mean the guy won't try again. The girls won't say anything, but they're nervous every time they fly, wondering if they're going to get hurt or worse."

"Then it's up to us to put a stop to the sabotage." He rubbed his hands together then got to his feet. "Ready? There's no time like the present."

Her breath hitched. Could she do this? Jasper wouldn't put her in danger. Nodding, she stood and grabbed her tray then followed him to the dish drop-off room. She dumped her items, and they hurried out of the building.

The heat slammed into her like a sauna, and she gasped. She would never get used to the scorching temperatures in Texas. Perspiration sprang to her forehead and trickled down her back. Striding ahead of her, Jasper seemed unaffected by the warmth. "Are we on a time crunch?"

He stopped and turned. "Sorry. No. The guy isn't off shift for another couple of hours, so he should be at the hangar. Guess I'm ready to have this nightmare over and done, so we can get on to doing important work toward winning the war."

"I'm with you, but I was sprinting to keep up with you." She grinned and put her hands on her hips. "I won't be any good to you if I'm gasping for breath when we get there."

"Good point. Hard to be undercover." He winked and waited for her to catch up.

Diverting her gaze from his sparkling moss-green eyes, she tucked her hands into her pockets and glanced toward their destination. Several large metal buildings hunched in the brown dirt at the entrance to the runways. Even though they were open to the elements, the relentless sun ensured the hangars' sauna-like conditions.

They continued their trek, and Evelyn caught sight of Jasper running his hand over his crew cut, a sure sign he was worried about what they were about to do. "Are you going to tell me my role in this little drama?"

"What? Oh, right." He shrugged. "I'm going to pretend I'm there to prepare for training and draw the guy into a conversation about you gals. My hope is that he'll confess...or at least give me some indication he's responsible for the incidents. You're to stay out of sight but close enough so you can hear what he says. Otherwise, it's my word against his."

"Do you really think he'll tell you what he's done? He's enlisted and you're an officer. Not like the two echelons are buddies."

"I don't know, but it's worth a try. I considered having Corporal Vance play the part, but I'm unsure of his acting abilities and thought he might blow the cover off the operation." He stopped and laid his hand on her arm. "See the mechanic working on the P-51? He's our man. Try to get behind the Vultee without him noticing you, and then I'll make a lot of noise as I approach him, so he'll focus on me."

Heart pounding in her throat, she nodded. All she had to do was listen. She tiptoed across the remaining distance to the aircraft and crouched behind the landing gear. Seconds later, Jasper passed her, whistling like a bird in springtime.

"Ho, there. Sergeant Siler, is it?" His deep voice echoed in the cavernous space. "Do you have a fifty-one I can borrow? I've got to spend some time doing remedial work with one of the gals."

A tool hit the ground with a clank. "Yeah, I'm Siler. There are two of 'em available. But do you really think tutoring her will help?" The man's nasal tone was condescending.

Evelyn rolled her eyes. No doubt as to his opinion, but did he hate the women enough to try to kill them?

Jasper snorted. "You got that right. Some of these gals aren't too smart, but I do the best I can with them. We've got some real lookers, but it bugs me to have them doing the jobs our boys should be doing. You know?"

"I hear you." A phlegmy cough, then Siler cleared his throat. "I definitely don't mind the scenery, but these dames belong at home, not here. I sure don't understand why Roosevelt thinks it's okay for them to be in the military."

"Technically, they're civilians."

"Whatever. They're getting in the way, and I wished they'd go home."

"Too bad they haven't been scared off yet."

The man grunted but didn't say anything, and silence fell.

Evelyn stifled the desire to peek around the landing gear. What was happening? Why didn't the man respond? Did he suspect Jasper was leading him into a trap?

"Wonder what else can be done to change their minds about doing their bit." Jasper's voice held a hard edge.

"I'm kind of surprised to hear you talkin' like this, sir. Some of the boys think you fancy one the those gals."

"They're correct. But just because I'm in love with Miss Reid, doesn't mean I want her here flying airplanes."

Evelyn licked her lips. Claiming to be in love with her was a nice touch. If she didn't know better, she'd be convinced Jasper believed the words he was spouting.

"You're in love, huh? Is that who's coming for extra *tutoring*?" An ugly laugh filled with insinuation spewed from the man's mouth.

"Nah, this session is for real, but the student won't be here for another fifteen minutes. That's why I showed up early. I was under the impression you could give me some ideas about how to dampen the girls' enthusiasm for the program. Nothing serious like that crash a few weeks ago. I don't want any part of that because killing them is bad form, but something serious enough to make them quit."

"Hey, I don't know where you got your information, but I had nothing to do with what's been happening. I just do my job and keep my head down. Do you think I'm guilty? Is that why you're here?" The man's voice rose to a squeak. "It's not me, I tell you. Corporal—"

A shot rang out. Someone moaned and hit the floor.

"Jas—"

Rough hands grabbed Evelyn from behind and gripped her in a viselike hold. The cold steel of a gun barrel pressed against her neck. "Try anything funny, and you'll join him."

Was Jasper dead? Had she missed the opportunity to declare her love for him?

Chapter Nineteen

With the echo of the gunshot still ringing in his ears, Jasper dodged behind the tool chest parked near the airplane. He fumbled for his gun, adrenaline surging through his body. "Evelyn! Are you all right?"

A muffled squeal sounded then the clatter of footsteps.

"She's fine, Captain MacPherson. For now."

Jasper's heart dropped, and he peered around the cabinet. Corporal Vance stood behind the landing gear of the P-51 with one arm holding Evelyn to his chest and the other hand aiming a gun at her head. The man had fooled them all with his act. He'd set up poor Sergeant Siler, who now lay writhing on the floor, a bloodstain blooming on his chest. At the rate he was bleeding, a miracle would be needed for him to survive. "Let her go, Alex. Don't make things worse than they already are. Put down the gun, and we can talk."

"Yeah, talk. Like everyone's been talking. Blah, blah, blah. They keep saying the war will be over soon, but the shooting continues. Men are still dying. They claim the women are going to be let go, but they're still here. If the girls don't leave, the boys can't come home." His voice broke, and he cleared his throat. "And they have to come home."

What was going on with the man? Jasper rubbed his forehead. The corporal's ramblings sounded unbalanced yet rooted in something or someone. Did he have a relative serving overseas he was worried about? His words sounded like his actions against the women were a means to an end rather than vengeance.

"We can work out the situation for you. Tell me what you need, and I'll make sure it happens. No more talking."

"I don't believe you. Throw down your weapon."

Jasper moved from behind the tool chest then laid his gun on the floor and held up his hands. He needed to show the corporal he could be trusted, but he felt naked without the pistol. "I'm telling the truth. I don't know what's bugging you, but if you tell me about the situation, I'll work with the CO to get it resolved. Killing people isn't the answer. Like you said."

"Killing is the only thing they know. They don't care about us. We're cannon fodder. The boys die, and more are sent to take their place. Too many lives lost."

"I can't help you until you help me by releasing Evelyn." Jasper sent what he hoped was a reassuring smile at Evie. Her ashen cheeks were streaked with tears, her eyes wide and frantic. Strands of raven-colored hair had come loose from her ponytail and hung in disarray around her face. He couldn't let her die. He needed her to remain calm. Vance would sense any agitation which might exacerbate the situation.

Without moving his head to alert the corporal of his intentions, he surveyed the surroundings. Any other day, the hangar would be full of mechanics and pilots. Why not now? Had God cleared the field to prevent needless injuries or death? *Well, God, it's just You and me, so let me know how to best proceed.*

He caught sight of the telephone on the wall near the entrance. Would the corporal let him make a call to bring the CO here for negotiations? He glanced at Evelyn again. She seemed to be watching his every move. Could he convey the idea of pretending to faint? His gun was still in reach. In his confusion, Alex hadn't told him to kick away the weapon. If Evelyn fell to the ground and created a distraction, could he gain control of the gun and shoot the man?

Corporal Vance was mumbling to himself, lost in his thoughts and delusions. Jasper pressed his lips together. The pathetic soldier needed help, not death, which is what would happen. Training dictated that all shots were to be made to kill, so simply wounding the young man was not an option.

Evelyn whimpered, and Alex shook her. "Shut up! You stupid girls are in the way, and you're the worst of them. Thinking you're better than everyone. Stepping out with the good captain here who also thinks he's the best." Spittle flew from his twisted mouth, and his face was mottled with red.

Jasper sent her an imperceptible shake of his head, piercing her eyes with his gaze. He held out his arms. "Take me instead, Alex. You don't want to do this. You don't want the girls here, so release Miss Reid, and she'll hightail it out of here. Won't you, Evelyn?"

She nodded, myriad emotions flitting across her face: fear, turmoil, and...something else...was it wrath? Was she mad at herself for being trapped a second time by the man or the corporal for accosting her? If she were angry, she might be able to help.

"No. She's not going anywhere. She special to you, which means I've got the upper hand." Corporal Vance waved the pistol as he spoke. "You'll do whatever I say."

"Yes, you're in charge. No question about that." Jasper pinned on what he hoped was a conciliatory smile. Apparently, no one was coming to their aid, so the solution was up to him. "Look, Alex, we can stand here all morning, or you can tell me what you want, and we can resolve this." Trying not to tremble, he tucked his hands in his pockets to appear unthreatening to the guy. Not exactly a move taught in his defense classes, but the disturbed young man in front of him wasn't playing by the rules, so Jasper wouldn't go by the book.

"Fine. I want my brother sent home. He's been wounded three times, and the big boys keep sending him back to fly more missions. He's the only one left besides me."

Jasper's stomach hollowed. Apparently, the guy had lost more than his fair share of family. "How many?" He swallowed against the lump that had formed. "How many brothers did you have, Alex?"

"Three. We were serving together until the Sullivans died, and they broke us up. But Ned and Warren got killed anyway, so we've got to save Donald." He frowned. "They weren't supposed to die. That's why Ned was sent to Italy and Warren to France."

"I'm sorry about your brothers, Alex. It's not fair to lose so many. Will you let me call the CO and ask him to get the paperwork in motion to bring Donald home?"

Indecision crossed the young man's face. "How long will that take?"

"I don't know, but Commander Lynch can order a rush. Perhaps your brother can be home by dinnertime on Thursday. How does that sound?"

"Too good to be true. I don't know where he is. Haven't gotten a letter in a couple of weeks. Maybe they already killed him." His expression darkened, and he jerked Evelyn closer. "A life for a life, Captain. If my brother's dead, your lovely girl must be sacrificed."

"No, wait." Jasper's breath hitched. "Don't jump to any conclusions. You know how long the mail takes. Your brother's letters are probably hung up at some sorting station. Please, let me contact the CO. I can't help you unless you allow me to make the call."

Corporal Vance barked a harsh laugh. "So you're not the big man you'd like everyone to think you are. Need the CO to handle this? Pfft. You're useless." He waved at the phone with his gun. "Fine. Make the call, but don't do anything stupid. Got it?"

"Absolutely." Now was his chance. The corporal had given him permission to move. If he could make Evie understand what he needed her to do, he would have a split second to grab his weapon and disable the man. *Please, God, make this work. I don't want to kill Alex, but I can't let him hurt Evelyn.* "Evie, everything's going to be okay. Understand?"

Lips trembling, she nodded.

"Just as hot, but this isn't anything like the time you and I hiked near Madison. Remember? Boy, that was quite a day."

"Stop talking and make the call or she gets it." Corporal Vance jabbed Evie's neck with the pistol.

Jasper's heart stuttered. "Okay! Don't shoot. I'm trying to calm my girlfriend. Surely, you can understand that. I didn't mean to annoy you."

"Whatever."

"Evie, I'm going to make the call. All right?"

Understanding dawned in her eyes, and a tentative smile tugged at the corners of her mouth.

His hands still in the air, he used his fingers to count down. Three. Two. One.

Evelyn went limp and bent over the corporal's arm. He lost his grip, and she fell to the ground. "What?" He stared at her prone form, his gun limp in his hand.

Jasper dropped to the floor, grabbed his pistol, and fired.

Corporal Vance's eyes widened, and his weapon tumbled to the floor. He grabbed his chest. Blood seeped between his splayed fingers. He coughed, his breath gurgling. His eyes clouded then rolled up into his head. He dropped to his knees then collapsed on top of Evelyn.

She squealed and struggled to get out from under the man's beefy form.

Racing forward, gun still in his grip in the event the corporal wasn't dead, Jasper kicked the abandoned weapon away then yanked on her assailant's arm to pull him off Evie. Fingers pressed to Alex's neck, where a pulse should have pounded, Jasper grimaced. He'd killed the poor soul. *Dear God, forgive me.*

Evelyn scrambled away from the corpse and sat on the floor, arms wrapped around her middle and tears streaming. "Is he...?"

"I'm afraid so." A wave of nausea swept over Jasper, and he swallowed the bile that threatened to appear. As a pilot, he'd done his fair share of killing, but never one of his own comrades. A casualty of the war that would go uncounted.

He staggered toward Evie then lowered himself to the floor and gathered her in his arms. She shuddered and pressed her face into his shoulder. "My brave girl. I hoped you'd understand my reference to the day we ran into the bear, and we had to play dead so he wouldn't perceive us as a threat. You did great, but I never should have involved you in this. I should have had one of the boys be my witness. Corporal Vance will get his wish. His brother is now the last surviving child and will probably get sent home."

Evelyn sniffled and extricated herself. "Thank you for saving me. I was so scared."

"But you kept your wits about you." He tucked a silky lock of hair behind her ear, and she trembled. "We need to get you to the infirmary so the doc can look you over."

"I'm all right. He didn't hurt me."

"Not physically, but I want to make sure you don't go into shock." He glanced at the corporal's body. "Now, I really do have to make a call. Can you stand?"

"I think so."

He got to his feet then helped her up and wrapped his arm around her waist. They walked toward the phone, her steps hesitant. He slowed his gait. She could have been killed, and her death would have been his fault. He'd been irresponsible. What did Corporal Vance say? That Jasper had to be the big man? The guy was right. Jasper's arrogance had led him to believe he could set up a sting operation and resolve the situation on his own. And now a man lay dead, and Evelyn had come within a fraction of losing her life.

Corporal Vance's delusions had caused him to wage a one-man war on the girls, but the incidents at Camp Davis were proof there were other soldiers and airmen who didn't want the WASP around. Would Evelyn be safe at her next assignment?

Her next assignment. She was leaving as soon as her orders came through. He couldn't lose her a second time.

Chapter Twenty

Chattering and giggles from the hallway filtered into Evelyn's room through the closed door. She'd finally received her orders and been stunned to discover she was headed to officer training school. Why the army had invested in hours of pursuit-plane training in her then decided not to use her right away was a mystery. Torn between the honor of being selected and disappointment at not being given a piloting assignment, she sighed. Did Jasper have anything to do with the military's decision?

On the cot, her suitcase lay open and half-filled. She needed to finish packing so she could get on the road. Well, in the air actually. The CO has approved her ferrying one of the P-51s to the base in Orlando where she'd be stationed. She opened the wardrobe, pulled clothes off the hangers, and tossed them onto the bed. She bent and retrieved her shoes from the floor. Tucking them inside the luggage, she nibbled on her lower lip.

Even though she'd only been in Brownsville for a couple of months, she'd miss her cubby and the girls. They'd all been warm and friendly. Gladys especially. Memories assailed Evelyn, so she clicked on the radio to push them away. The Song Spinners belted out "Coming in on a Wing and a Prayer."

Perfect. An appropriate send-off. She tapped her foot as she collected her cosmetics, brush, toothbrush, and the rest of her personal effects and stuffed them into the quilted bag her mother had given her as a going-away present. She stowed the bag into her suitcase then folded her extra uniform and civvies and added them to the luggage.

She yanked open all the drawers to ensure she'd left nothing behind. The surfaces of the furniture were vacant, giving the room a sterile appearance. Ready for the next gal.

The door burst open, and Gladys stood on the threshold, her face flushed and her hair in disarray. "You weren't going to leave without saying goodbye, were you?"

"No, but I needed solitude." She shuddered and rubbed her arms. "I don't want to admit it, but yesterday's incident still has me rattled. I could have been killed, or Jasper."

"I can't believe what happened." She rushed forward and hugged Evelyn. "I mean, the guy was a little creepy the few times I saw him, but it never occurred to me he was the saboteur. And he's not the only one who hates us." She pulled a newspaper clipping from her pocket and held it out.

Evelyn took the paper and glanced at the title: "Women Pilots Unnecessary and Undesirable." She scanned the article then frowned.

"Another scathing piece full of misinformation about the WASP. How can *Time* call itself a news periodical if it doesn't bother to fact check?"

Gladys shrugged. "They're not the only ones. Ever since Congress started talking about making us part of the military, there's been a campaign to discredit us. Sometimes I wonder if staying in the program is worth it. Why should I stay somewhere I'm not wanted?"

"I've been having second thoughts, too. Especially since I'm not going to be flying anytime soon." She shook her head then closed the latches on the suitcase and set it on the floor. She dropped onto the bed.

Curling her legs up under herself, Gladys joined her. "You know, it might serve them right if we all resigned. They'd figure out how much work we've been doing for them."

"Maybe not. Supposedly, there are thousands of men who have been freed up and can now perform the job we're doing. Most of them are afraid of being transferred to the walking army as they're calling it."

"Yeah, well, they should have thought of that possibility when they turned down lower-paying ferrying jobs at the beginning of the war."

"Hindsight being what it is, I'm sure they've already considered that." Evelyn raked her fingers through her hair. "Did you read *Time's* article last month calling Jackie Cochran an ex-beauty shop operator?"

"I missed that one." Gladys gestured to the clipping Evelyn had put on the dresser. "Sure wish we'd get the respect we deserve."

"True, and maybe we will someday, but for now, we can be proud of our accomplishments and not have to worry about any man's opinion."

Evelyn rubbed her hands together. "Now, let's do something fun before I shove off."

"Have you already said goodbye to Jasper?" Gladys cocked her head. "He saved your life. I figured you'd spend your last couple of hours with him."

"I know, but it would be too hard. I'd rather have time with you and the girls."

Gladys narrowed her eyes. "Did you tell him how you feel? You can't leave without doing that."

"Why not?" Evelyn's chest tightened. What her friend didn't know what that seeing Jasper would cause Evelyn's resolve to remain aloof to crumble, and she couldn't let that happen.

"Because it's not fair to him. Or you. I've seen the two of you together. You love each other. Deeply. And to let opinions divide you seems ridiculous to me. You're throwing away a chance at something special that many people would give anything to have."

"I know." Tears pricked the backs of Evelyn's eyes. "I'm conflicted, but the war can't last forever, so we can try again afterwards."

"Nonsense." Gladys stood. "You need to find Jasper and tell him. Now. Otherwise, this opportunity will be lost forever. And you'll regret it for the rest of your life. Take if from someone who knows."

"What—"

Shaking her head, Gladys opened the door. "That's all I'm going to say." Her lips trembled. "The girls and I will be sunning behind the barracks. I hope you'll stop by before you leave." She left the room and closed the door with a firm click.

Evelyn stared at the space her friend had vacated and blew out a deep breath. She already regretted her decision. Her stomach roiled at the thought of leaving Jasper behind, but pursuing a relationship was too dangerous. His expectations of the perfect wife didn't line up with hers, and she might be happy initially, but eventually, she'd come to resent him. A clean break so they could move on with their lives was the best thing.

Maybe she should resign and return to her crop dusting business. With the brouhaha associated with the program, the military was sure to disband the WASP at some point. Why not get a jump on the inevitable and leave the program on her own terms? Quitting would ensure she'd never see Jasper again. Why didn't that thought give her any peace?

"Gladys, have you seen Evelyn?" Jasper started to run his hand over his crew cut then lowered his arm. A nervous habit he needed to stop.

"She didn't track you down?"

"No, was she supposed to?"

Gladys huffed out a breath and frowned. "I thought I'd convinced her, but you know how stubborn she can be."

"That I do." He glanced at his watch. If he didn't find her soon, she'd fly out of his life without so much as a by-your-leave. Is that what she wanted? Should he give her the chance to flee? His stomach hollowed.

No. God had allowed her to come back into his life. He was sure of it even if Evie wasn't. "I tried the barracks and the mess hall. Where else could she be?"

"In a plane?"

He shook his head. "She's not scheduled to leave for another hour, so she doesn't need to head to the hangar for thirty more minutes."

"Unless she's trying to avoid us."

"She hasn't said goodbye to you either?"

"I had a few minutes with her while she was packing, but when I told her to speak with you, she put me off."

"Why did you tell her to talk to me?"

Gladys tugged on her ear. "It's not my place to say, but if I were you, I'd hotfoot it to the hangar. Even if she's not there now, she'll show up eventually." She laid her hand on his arm. "Be gentle, Jasper. For some reason she's as fearful as a rescued pup, but I think you have a chance."

He stared at her long and hard, pulse surging. Was she telling him that Evelyn cared more than she let on? That she loved him enough to...no, he wouldn't go there. Not until he'd had a chance to look into her eyes. Their crystal-blue depths would tell him what he needed to know.

She winked and gave him a gentle shove. "Times a-wasting, man. Get going."

"You're right. What am I waiting for?" He grabbed her in a quick embrace. "Thanks, Gladys. You're the best."

"I'll bet you say that to all the girls." She giggled as she waved and walked away.

The sun beat down on his head, and his shirt stuck to his back like a second skin as he hurried toward the hangar. Why hadn't he thought to meet her there? "You know exactly why, old man, and you better pull yourself together if you plan to convince Evie of your unconditional love."

"Sir?"

Jasper's head whipped toward the voice. A private, who couldn't be more than eighteen years old, stared at him in confusion. He's been so intent on his mission, he hadn't seen the young man who apparently thought Jasper had been speaking to him. "Carry on, soldier."

"Yes, sir." With a look of relief, the boy saluted and continued past.

Great. The kid probably thought he was shell-shocked. Jasper hunched forward as he strode toward his destination. The wind gusted sending dust into the air. He coughed and covered his nose and mouth with one hand. Texas had a lot going for it, but he could live without the constant grit.

The sound of metal on metal mingled with conversation and laughter filtered out the open door. Several planes sat outside the hanger, their canopies open and ready for pilots. He surveyed the aircraft. All empty. Was Evie inside?

He jogged into the hangar and stopped. Three planes. Three mechanics. No Evelyn. He hurried to the nearest guy. "Say, I'm looking for Evelyn Reid. She's scheduled to ferry a P-51 in about an hour. Has she arrived yet?"

The mechanic waved his wrench toward the taxiway. "She received permission for an earlier takeoff, so she's already on her way."

Jasper looked over his shoulder and cringed. A gleaming P-51 trundled across the macadam toward the runway. "No. She can't go."

"You could call the tower to request an abort."

"Yeah...uh...thanks." To ask the controllers to scrub or delay her flight for a personal reason was a serious breach of protocol. He and Evie would both get in trouble. Shoulders slumped, he walked out of the hangar. The aircraft continued to roll toward the departure lane. A jeep sat next to the Vultee, and he grinned. He whirled and raced back inside. "Hey, can I borrow that jeep?"

The man shrugged. "Sure, but—"

"Thanks." Jasper ran out of the building and leapt into the vehicle. He started the engine and roared toward the departing aircraft. Faster. Must go faster. Would the plane outpace him before he could get her attention?

He pressed on the accelerator, and the jeep shot forward. He was gaining on her. His heart pounded, and his breath came in gasps.

Thirty yards.

Twenty yards.

Ten yards.

Finally, he was even with the wings of the plane, its engines deafening. She'd never hear him if he called to her. He drew alongside the cockpit and flailed his right arm while keep his left hand gripped to the wheel. One wrong move, and he'd flip the vehicle or be crushed by the landing gear.

He looked toward the cockpit.

Evelyn was staring at him, astonishment etched on her face.

"Evelyn, stop the plane." He shouted even though he knew she couldn't hear him. Maybe she could read his lips. Or maybe chasing her had scared the daylights out of her.

She shook her head and waved him away. "Go away," she mouthed.

"Please, stop." He pressed his hand against his chest then held up his hand. "Five minutes. Just give me five minutes." Neck and neck, they careened down the runway.

Then it happened.

The shrill whine of the engine lessened. Seconds later, the aircraft began to slow. He let his foot off the accelerator to keep pace with the plane as it reduced speed. Evie spoke into her mouthpiece.

His heart leapt in his chest. She must be notifying the tower of her intention to abort the takeoff. The jeep sputtered then caught. His gaze shot to the dash. Had he run out of gas? No. The one-hundred-and-thirty-five degree angle of the temperature gauge needle told him the engine was overheating. She'd agreed to stop none too soon.

Tires rumbling, the plane's momentum continued to decelerate until coming to rest nearly halfway down the runway.

Evelyn opened the canopy and squinted at him.

Jasper crawled out of the jeep. His legs quivered like jelly, and his muscles protested as he climbed onto the wing. His pulse erratic, he took a big breath. He had her attention. Now what?

"Jasp—"

"Evie—"

"You first." She gave him a wry smile. "After all, you're the one who flagged me down."

His face warmed, and he ducked his head.

She snorted a laugh. "Since when are you shy?"

"Since I've got one last chance to make things right between us." He straightened his spine and took her hand. "Thanks for stopping. I was almost too late, and the Willy almost conked out, but we made it."

She tilted her head and quirked one eyebrow.

"Right. Get to the point." He leaned forward so he could see into her eyes as he spoke. Her mouth might say one thing, but her clear blue eyes would tell him what she thought. "Evie, I love you. I always have. My life is empty without you, and I want to be the man you need me to be."

"But—"

He put his index finger against her lips. "Please, let me finish. I know I've made a ton of mistakes, too many to count, but I've come to realize I've been a fool, an arrogant, self-important dunce who tried to mold you into someone I thought you should be." He frowned. "Which is ridiculous. Why change the woman I fell in love with? You had every right to hate me."

"Jasper."

"Wait. Anyway, I'm sorry for how I treated you. I love you just as you are. An intelligent, bold, beautiful *pilot.* Please say you'll give me a second chance and agree to be my wife."

Her ice-blue gaze softened, then her eyes filled with tears that tumbled down her cheeks. Her chin trembled. She laced her fingers with his and nodded. "Yes." Her voice broke. "I can't fight my feelings any longer. I love you, Jasper. I saw the changes in you, but I didn't believe them. I was afraid of falling for you again and getting hurt."

"Then why did you say yes?"

"Because any man crazy enough to chase a P-51 down the runway must care for me a bit."

Jasper threw back his head and guffawed. "Just a bit." He leaned over the edge of the cockpit and pressed a warm kiss to her mouth. Oh, to hold her in his arms and give her a proper embrace. He pulled back and tapped her nose. "This isn't the romantic setting I had in mind when I rehearsed this moment."

She giggled, and her eyes sparkled in the sunlight. "You've been practicing?"

His heart full, he grinned. "I know you have to leave, and I'll miss you terribly, but I'll be waiting for however long I need, my flygirl." He kissed her again then stroked her jaw with his thumb. She captured his hand and kissed his palm.

He jumped off the wing and crawled behind the wheel of the jeep. The temperature gauge was back to normal, but he couldn't say the same about his own. His pulse raced, and he had no doubt he was grinning like a fool.

She lowered the canopy and spoke into her headset then guided the aircraft toward runway two and was soon airborne. High overhead, she dipped one wing, and he waved his arms until the plane roared out of sight.

Waiting would seem interminable, but she deserved to fulfill her commitment and to live her dream. Daylight was burning. He better get started on the first of many letters telling his bride-to-be how proud he was of her.

Epilogue

Snow swirled outside the window as Evelyn paced in the small room adjacent to the church foyer. Her ivory-colored suit rustled as she walked. Music from the organ filtered through the wall. Somewhere in the recesses of the building, Jasper waited. The quintessential pilot with nerves of steel, was he taking their wedding day in stride or was he as nervous as she was?

She checked her reflection in the mirror for the umpteenth time then smoothed her skirt. Not that there were wrinkles, but the motion gave her something to do. Had the weather deterred her guests? As long as there were a couple of witnesses, she didn't need a crowd.

Her engagement ring glinted in the lights, and she studied the brilliant stone. A few weeks after her arrival in Orlando, Jasper had visited and taken her to a remote park to propose again. Properly, as he said. He'd gotten down on one knee and declared his love then presented the beautiful ring.

Officers' training had been interesting, and she'd done well, then been assigned to California. A huge base that gave her an opportunity to fly nearly every plane used by the air force. She'd settled in and made lots of friends but missed Jasper more than she imagined she could. He wrote almost daily, his letters filled with stories about the incoming classes of female pilots. Time passed quickly, and she racked up lots of hours in the air, but by fall she was tiring of the job. Her heart ached from her desire to see Jasper. She loved to fly. But she loved him more.

In October, General Arnold released a memo announcing the deactivation of the WASP program. His praise of the women and their contribution to the war effort was gracious, but the fact they were no longer needed stung. Many of the girls had quit immediately after receiving the notification, but she'd remained until the bitter end. What would she do now that she didn't have planes to fly?

The door opened, and her father poked his head inside. "You ready, honey?"

Her heart flip-flopped, and she nodded. She turned back to the mirror, straightened the pillbox hat on her head, then pulled the short veil over her face. "Ready."

"You're a lovely bride, Evelyn. I hope you'll be very happy." His gaze pierced her eyes. "Say the word, and we can duck out the back door."

She laid her hand on his arm and smiled. "Jasper is a good man, Dad. I trust him, and you can to."

"If you say so, but he hurt my little girl."

"That was a long time ago. We both said and did things we shouldn't, but we're starting fresh, and the difference is there are three of us in the relationship now. Our faith in God has grown, and we realize we left Him out the first time around." She kissed his cheek. "I love you, Dad. Thanks for looking out for me. I've always been able to count on your love and support. No matter what."

Moisture sprang to his eyes, and he cleared his throat. "And that will continue even after your marriage." He held out his arm, and she slipped her hand in the crook of his elbow. They left the room and took their place at the back of the sanctuary. Music swelled as they walked toward the front of the church.

She caught sight of Jasper, and the expressions of friends and family blurred as she focused on his face, wreathed in smiles. Her own smile was wide as she approached her beloved. Only God knew what her future held, but with Jasper by her side anything was possible. She and her father arrived at the altar, and he placed her hand in Jasper's then lifted her veil.

Jasper squeezed her fingers, and she sighed with contentment. They turned toward the pastor, and the next chapter of her life began with his words, "Friends, we are gathered here today to witness the joining of two people: Evelyn Margaret Reid and Jasper Aiden MacPherson..."

It seemed like only moments passed when the ceremony neared its end. The preacher nodded at Jasper. "You may now kiss your bride."

"Gladly." Jasper winked and lowered his head, pressing his lips to hers.

Their breath mingled, and her toes curled. Tingles shot up her spine. Her heart soared higher than she'd ever flown.

THE END

What did you think of *Love at First Flight?*

Thank you so much for purchasing *Love at First Flight*. You could have selected any number of books to read, but you chose this book.

I hope it added encouragement and exhortation to your life. If so, it would be nice if you could share this book with your family and friends by posting to Facebook (www.facebook.com) and/or Twitter (www.twitter.com).

If you enjoyed this book and found some benefit in reading it, I'd appreciate it if you could take some time to post a review on Amazon, Goodreads, Kobo, GooglePlay, Apple Books, or other book review site of your choice. Your feedback and support will help me to improve my writing craft for future projects and make this book even better.
Thank you again for your purchase.

Blessings,
Linda Shenton Matchett

Acknowledgments

Although writing a book is a solitary task, it is not a solitary journey. There have been many who have helped and encouraged me along the way.

My parents, Richard and Jean Shenton, who presented me with my first writing tablet and encouraged me to capture my imagination with words. Thanks, Mom and Dad!

Scribes212 – my ACFW online critique group: Valerie Goree, Marcia Lahti, and the late Loretta Boyett (passed on to Glory, but never forgotten). Without your input, my writing would not be nearly as effective.

Eva Marie Everson – my mentor/instructor with Christian Writers' Guild. You took a timid, untrained student and turned her into a writer. Many thanks!

SincNE, and the folks who coordinate the Crimebake Writing Conference. I have attended many writing conferences, but without a doubt, Crimebake is one of the best. The workshops, seminars, panels, critiques, and every tiny aspect are well-executed, professional, and educational.

Special thanks to Hank Phillippi Ryan, Halle Ephron, and Roberta Isleib for your encouragement and spot-on critiques of my work.

Thanks to my Book Brigade who provide information, encouragement, and support.

Paula Proofreader (https://paulaproofreader.wixsite.com/home): I'm so glad I found you! My work is cleaner because of your eagle eye. Any mistakes are completely mine.

A heartfelt thank you to my brothers, Jack Shenton and Douglas Shenton, and my sister, Susan Shenton Greger for being enthusiastic cheerleaders during my writing journey. Your support means more than you'll know.

My husband, Wes, deserves special kudos for understanding my need to write. Thank you for creating my writing room – it's perfect, and I'm thankful for it every day. Thank you for your willingness to accept a house that's a bit cluttered, laundry that's not always done, and meals on the go. I love you.

And finally, to God be the glory. I thank Him for giving me the gift of writing and the inspiration to tell stories that shine the light on His goodness and mercy.

Want more romance? Read on for the first chapter of *Spies & Sweethearts, Sisters in Service, book 1*.

Chapter One

Just because she was the eldest, did Cora have to criticize Emily's every decision? She was a high school French teacher, not a schoolgirl. Shaking her head, Emily climbed on the bike and pedaled away from the house. She'd exhausted her gas rations for the week, so using the car was out. Fortunately, the library wasn't far. She could finish preparing the end-of-year exams there.

Two of her students were already gone. Days after they turned eighteen, the boys talked the principal into letting them graduate early in order to enlist. Her heart constricted. Now, both were in training with the army air force and would soon be on their way overseas to fight the Germans. They spoke French impeccably, a skill better used in the ambassador ranks rather than on an airplane.

The warm air stroked Emily's cheeks as she rode. Squinting against the sun's glare, she huffed out a breath. At least the boys were doing something for the war effort. Her service with the American Women's Voluntary Services as a plane spotter and messenger wasn't exactly going to turn the tide against the Axis powers. Surely, there was something more she could do.

She braked in front of the sandstone building and wheeled her bike into an empty spot in one of the racks near the entrance of Trafalgar Public Library. A Carnegie library, it housed several hundred books thanks to the Scottish-American philanthropist. What would he think of the war?

"Emily!"

A broad grin on her face, Joan Boyer hurried toward Emily. Her floral dress danced around her leg, and her ponytail flounced. "Your mom said I'd find you here." Her smile faltered. "Are you okay? You look terrible."

"Gee, thanks. Glad I can count on you for support."

"What?"

Emily finger-combed her hair. "I'm sorry. I had another argument with Cora. Just because she's already been married and widowed, she thinks she knows what's good for everyone."

Joan linked her arm through Emily's. "Let's grab a seat in the memorial garden. You can tell me everything."

They sauntered to the wooden bench sheltered by a large, weeping cherry tree and surrounded by black-eyed Susans, and a rainbow of coneflowers and petunias nodding in the breeze.

"All right. What gives? You've been annoyed with Cora in the past, but you seem especially angry today."

"I am." Emily slumped against the seat. "True or not, it feels like neither she nor Doris take me seriously because I'm the youngest. That all I'm good enough for is teaching a bunch of kids. A few days ago, Cora commented that plane spotting night duty must be interfering with my job, and she didn't understand why I was still volunteering. Like I can't juggle multiple responsibilities. I'm almost twenty-six years old. I'm quite capable."

"Maybe she worries about you."

"Perhaps, but it doesn't seem like concern. It feels like criticism of my life." Emily fisted her hands. "This morning, I got a letter telling me I've been accepted into a new government program. I leave for training the day after school is out. She overheard me telling Mom about the job and quizzed me about it. When I told her I couldn't share specifics, she rolled her eyes and asked what the government needed with a schoolteacher."

"That's awful." Joan squeezed Emily's shoulder.

"The worst of it is that once she got started down that road, Mom followed…said I should rethink the opportunity…that I have a perfectly good job here at home, and my volunteer work is sufficient." She frowned. "Then Mom said I'm being selfish to go off on my own. It's bad enough I'm still living at home at my age, but for them to try to dictate my decisions is too much."

"What are you going to do?"

"Send a telegram accepting the position. I've got to live my own life no matter what they say." She blinked away tears forming in her eyes. "Do you think I'm being self-centered by going?"

"Absolutely not. Your parents are in perfect health, and Cora is living here, too. She can take care of any needs they might have." Joan leaned forward. "You really can't say much about the job? Not even a little?"

The tightness in Emily's chest eased, and she chuckled. "You always could make me feel better. I'm sorry for not telling you I applied, but I was skeptical I'd get selected. You should have seen the crowd. Anyway, I don't know a lot about the job. There is a new governmental department, and it needs people who are bilingual. The exam contained lots of translation exercises, especially with regard to colloqialisms and dialect for different regions in France and French-speaking countries."

"Now you know how your students feel."

"Absolutely, but that doesn't mean I'm going to go easy on them for the final." Emily rubbed her damp palms on her skirt. "I can't believe this will be my last year of teaching for a while…maybe forever. I'm a bit nervous about notifying the principal about leaving. The factories pay much higher than the schools, so Medford has had a lot of resignations. The school may have to combine classes next year."

"This war won't last forever. In fact, some say it will be over by Christmas. Surely you'll be back."

Emily shook her head. "I don't want to be a naysayer, but I doubt the war will be over by the end of the year. I think we're in this for the long haul."

"Can you at least tell me where you're going? I could come visit."

"I've forgotten the address, somewhere in Washington, DC, but that's not my final stop. I'll be transported with other new employees to the training facility where I'll stay for three months. I won't be able to send or receive letters while I'm there. And definitely no visitors."

Joan bolted upright. "That sounds intriguing, very secretive. If you're lucky, there will be a few dreamboats in the class."

"Romance is the last thing I need, Joan. Besides, guys our age are in the defense industry or armed forces. There won't be anyone to fall in love with."

Gerard Lucas resisted the urge to run a finger around the collar of his dress uniform to loosen the stifling piece of clothing. What he wouldn't give to be in a flannel shirt and pair of overalls. Out in the field, wind ruffling his hair, and acres of crops flourishing in the sunshine. Perhaps a beautiful woman by his side. And—

"Lieutenant Lucas, are you listening to me?"

Gerard wrenched his thoughts back to the present and snapped his heels together. "Sir, yes, sir."

"Insulting and then arguing with a higher ranking officer in front of his men and the local Brits is a serious offense. The only things keeping you out of the brig or a dishonorable discharge are this war and the fact you didn't take a poke at him. The country needs all the men we can get." Major Albert shook his head. "You're a bright guy, one who should be climbing the ranks rather than getting demoted every three months. You are lucky Major Quigley had you reduced to private."

"Sir, he didn't know what he was talking about—"

"I did not give you permission to speak, and therein lies your problem. Failure to respect the chain of command. You are to obey orders without question and to show respect to those ranked above you. You're arrogant and argumentative. More than a few officers have made that observation. Not a good combination, Lucas." The major dropped into the chair behind his desk. "You need to apologize to Major Quigley. In public. At the pub where the incident occurred."

"Yes, sir."

"Excellent. Now, the good news for everyone is that you are being transferred to an intelligence unit based out of Washington, DC. Apparently, your penchant for getting into trouble is a desirable trait to them."

Gerard's heart sped up. There'd been stories about guerrilla warfare and espionage, but he figured the information was rumor, like most of what he heard in between training exercises. Was he finally going to see the war up close? Or rather, behind the scenes?

Major Albert tossed him a set of papers then gestured to the vacant chair. "At ease, Soldier."

Dropping into the seat, Gerard tugged at his collar and sighed. The material still scratched his skin and threatened to suffocate him. He picked his orders and scanned the instructions. He had two days to prepare. To wait and wonder what was in store for him.

"As you can see, you leave the day after tomorrow. Unless you run into a hitch, you'll report for duty on Saturday. Try not to mess this up. It may be your last chance to remain a free man."

"Permission to speak candidly, sir?"

"I'd expect nothing less, Lucas."

"Why me?"

"Why you, what?"

"You must have recommended me, sir. Otherwise, how would they know about me?" Gerard studied the major. "So why did you put my name forward for consideration?"

"It appears I haven't underestimated your abilities. You're right. I did recommend you." Major Albert smirked. "This new department…they're calling it the Office of Strategic Services…a positively bureaucratic label, if you ask me, but maybe that's what they want everyone to think. Personally, from the bits and pieces I've been able to glean, it's more like the department of dirty tricks. Anyway, that sounded like something you'd be suited for. You know, swimming against the tide."

"I appreciate your faith in me, sir. I won't let you down."

"It's not me I'm worried about. Don't let yourself down, Lucas. You've got to come to terms with whatever's eating you. Yes, you don't suffer fools, and that's fine, but it's more than that. You're carting around a lot of anger. Maybe you know why. Maybe you don't. Either way, you need to channel those feelings or jettison them, because if you don't, you'll get yourself killed. Understood?"

"Yes, sir."

Major Albert steepled his fingers. "Quigley wanted to bring you up on charges, put you through a court-martial, but I talked him out of it."

"Thank you, sir."

"I'm not looking for gratitude. I'm telling you because this is your last chance. Not everyone is willing to accept your shenanigans. And despite the roguish nature of your new assignment, there will be some sort of hierarchy. Adhere to it, or you may not survive this war." He rose and extended his hand. "Good luck, son, and Godspeed."

They shook hands. Gerard put on his peaked wool cap, saluted, then pivoted and hurried from the room, a grin tugging at his lips. Finally, a chance to avenge his brother's death in the Atlantic at the hands of a German submarine wolfpack.

Other Titles
Romance

Love's Harvest, Wartime Brides, Book 1

Love's Rescue, Wartime Brides, Book 2

Love's Belief, Wartime Brides, Book 3

Love's Allegiance, Wartime Brides, Book 4

Love Found in Sherwood Forest

A Love Not Forgotten

On the Rails

A Doctor in the House (The Hope of Christmas Collection)

Spies & Sweethearts, Sisters in Service, Book 1

The Mechanic & the MD, Sisters in Service, Book 2

The Widow & the War Correspondent, Sisters in Service, Book 3

Dinah's Dilemma (Westward Home $ Hearts Mail-Order Brides Book 10)

Mystery
Under Fire, Ruth Brown Mystery Series, Book 1

Under Ground, Ruth Brown Mystery Series, Book 2

Under Cover, Ruth Brown Mystery Series, Book 3

Murder of Convenience, Women of Courage, Book 1

Murder at Madison Square Garden, Women of Courage, Book 2

Non-Fiction
WWII Word Find, Volume 1

Biography

Linda Shenton Matchett writes about ordinary people who did extraordinary things in days gone by. She is a volunteer docent and archivist at the Wright Museum of WWII and a trustee for her local public library. Born in Baltimore, Maryland, a stone's throw from Fort McHenry, she has lived in historical places most of her life. Now located in central New Hampshire, Linda's favorite activities include exploring historic sites and immersing herself in the imaginary worlds created by other authors.

Website/blog: http://www.LindaShentonMatchett.com
Facebook: http://www.facebook.com/LindaShentonMatchettAuthor
Pinterest: http://www.pinterest.com/lindasmatchett
Amazon: https://www.amazon.com/Linda-Shenton-Matchett/e/B01DNB54S0
Goodreads: http://www.goodreads.com/author_linda_matchett
Bookbub: http://www.bookbub.com/authors/linda-shenton-matchett